OPERATOR 5: WHEN HELL CAME TO AMERICA

WHEN HELL CAME TO AMERICA

By Curtis Steele

POPULAR PUBLICATIONS • 2024

PUBLISHING HISTORY

"When Hell Came to America" originally appeared in the January/February, 1939 (Vol. 11, No. 3) issue of *Operator #5* magazine. Copyright © 2024 by Argosy Communications, Inc. All rights reserved.

CHAPTER 1
DEATH STRIKES

TIMES SQUARE was ablaze with light, a great splash of multi-colored, flashing, blinking radiance that overflowed the heart of New York's theatrical district and trickled into the side streets until the surrounding darkness closed in and blanketed it. The sidewalks were crowded with people, the streets filled with taxicabs and private cars. It was not quite seven-thirty, but already the square was pulsing and throbbing with the quickening tempo of gay nightlife as the traffic arteries poured additional thousands into the pleasure center of the world.

People were everywhere—crowds hurrying to and from restaurants; crowds debating the attractions of rival motion picture theaters; crowds loitering in front of store windows; crowds just walking in that seemingly endless treadmill that is Broadway at night.

Life going on....

Two in that moving throng walked more quickly than most of the others—or at least one of them did. So impatiently, in fact, that his companion grabbed his arm and held him back, as they hurried up Seventh Avenue toward the jammed square.

"Take it easy—take it easy!" Ralph Kennedy chuckled. "She won't run away from you. You're engaged to her now, old man. You've got to start asserting a little independence."

He laughed.

"But we're late," Phil Dawson protested, as he glanced at his wrist-watch. "We were supposed to meet the girls at seven-thirty. If you hadn't taken so confoundedly long—"

"Almost *ten minutes* late!" Kennedy jeered. "Engaged less than twenty-four hours—and here he is running around like a worried old hen-pecked husband! Don't blame me. We'd have made it if you hadn't insisted on stopping for these gorgeous corsages."

Kennedy's eyes twinkled as he watched his friend's eagerness. Phil Dawson and Harriet Loomis were going to be happy—no doubt about that. They were very much in love, and had been for years. Last night they had announced their engagement, and tonight was to be the engagement celebration—a little dinner party with Kennedy and Evelyn Harvey, who in a few months time were to be their best man and bridesmaid. A perfect match, if ever Kennedy had seen one....

"There they are—over there beside the Times Building!" Dawson exclaimed, as his searching eyes picked out the figure of his sweetheart from more than a block away. "I'll bet they were there before seven-fifteen—"

The rest of that sentence was never uttered. It was blasted back into his throat by a terrific explosion that seemed to rend the whole world apart! An explosion that swept everything before it—that hurled Kennedy and Dawson back as if a great hand had whipped them off their feet!

Fully twenty-five feet they were flung through the air before they hit the sidewalk and rolled into the gutter. Dazed, hardly able to breathe, they lay there gasping. Then Kennedy got to

Times Square was being torn apart!

his hands and knees, to his feet. Groggily he shook his head. Everything inside his skull seemed to be buzzing, as if a great rumbling were pressing down on him. A dull, muffled rumble that seemed to come from overhead....

He looked up at the sky, but it was black and impenetrable. If there was anything up there, the darkness shrouded it completely.

Now Dawson was on his feet, also—was batting his eyes incredulously as he stared in the direction of the square, a block away.

"My God—they're gone!" suddenly burst from his lips. "Everyone's gone! *Harriet!*"

Kennedy stared, too, and what he saw amazed him—sent an eerie, shivery chill along his spine. Times Square was almost dark, the flooding illumination all but extinguished—and it was utterly bare of people! The crowds that had been there a few moments before....

From the corner of his eye Kennedy caught a glimpse of something moving, something that grasped his attention. His gaze flashed back to his immediate surroundings. There, just across the corner from him, an automobile was parked on Forty-first Street, its bumper barely even with the Seventh Avenue building line. Three men were getting out of the car—three men who strode the few steps to the avenue and stared in the direction of Times Square, just as he and Dawson had been doing.

But there was a difference. These men were not astounded, were not horrified—they were gloating! And suddenly Kennedy knew that they realized exactly what they would see there—that they had been *expecting* it!

One of them stood in a position so that the night-light burning inside the corner bank fell full upon his face—the face of a thin-featured, broad-foreheaded man. A vulpine face—with the eyes slitted, the lips drawn back tightly from white teeth. A face that Kennedy would never forget.

That much he saw in the flash of a second as a subconscious, instinctive warning whirled him around—and then they saw him and Dawson. Instantly their hands darted to their coats, and orange flashes spurted from them. The strangely silenced street echoed with the crackle of shots. A pane of glass shattered just behind Kennedy—and then Phil Dawson gasped and tottered uncertainly, only to be flung to the ground when a second and third bullet ripped into his body.

Kennedy flung himself down beside his friend, grasped the inert head and turned it so that he could look at the face, at the sagging jaw and staring eyes. Phil Dawson was dead—and he would be dead, too, in another moment.

But Kennedy didn't want to die. Hot rage flooded him and he wanted to come to grips with those murderous devils, wanted to tear them to pieces. That was folly, without a weapon of any sort. Just as foolish as kneeling there and being killed—and never having a chance to even this grim score for poor Phil....

THOSE THOUGHTS were subconscious.... They flashed through Kennedy's mind and brought an instantaneous reaction. Springing up from beside the body of his friend, he raced fifty feet and dived into a subway entrance. Down the steps he tore, but even before he whisked through the turnstile he heard the pursuing footsteps clattering after him.

Through a passageway that led to the maze of Times Square platforms he sped, with the blasting of shots close behind him spurring him to greater efforts. Those killers were gaining on him. Any moment now a bullet might bring him down—unless he could reach help.

But there seemed to be no help....

Suddenly he realized that the busy station was strangely silent—muted as a tomb. And then he almost pitched headlong over the body of a woman lying right in his path. A woman, then two men—and then dozens of them. The platform was littered with corpses—yet not only the platform. A train stood beside it, the doors open. The conductor who should have operated it now sprawled between two cars. A dead man—in charge of a trainload of corpses!

Kennedy's eyes fairly bugged from his head as he looked at those lighted cars with their rows of passengers slumped in their seats—and in that moment came the inspiration that proved his salvation. Darting through one of the open doors, he dropped into a vacant seat and slumped like the corpse that was his neighbor.

Down the platform he heard his pursuers pound, heard them cursing and calling to one another. Then once more the deathly quiet settled over him—quiet that was soon broken by the impatient, querulous whistle of a train that had come in behind the death-laden one and could not enter the station. Not until he heard the motorman shouting from his window, heard the train's doors open and men surge out onto the platform, did he dare to leave his unmoving companions.

Slipping out of the death car, he hurried to a stairway and went up into Times Square. Then he stood paralyzed with horror at the ghastly sights that met his eyes on every side!

Times Square was a place of the dead. The sidewalks were piled with corpses—corpses that had been hurled against the buildings and through the windows into the stores. The streets were a mad tangle of overturned and wrecked automobiles scattered in wildest confusion. Where a few minutes before there had been thousands of laughing, chatting people starting out for an evening of entertainment—now there was nothing but grim, stark death!

Blindly Times Square looked down at the appalling horror. For not a window on any side boasted a pane of glass—not a bulb or neon tube-studded display sign that had not been shattered and darkened. From the upper windows of some of the buildings light shone out over the shambles, and from three or four blocks away the gay signs still blazed and flickered—a touch of normalcy that seemed strange and indecent in that grisly charnel-place.

But now Ralph Kennedy was no longer alone. Men were surging in from the side streets; cars were coming in from Broadway and from Seventh Avenue. Police whistles were shrilling, sirens wailing. The silence of the tomb gave way to the babble of horrified men, the shrieks of hysterical women. It became a panicky uproar.

Kennedy's eyes narrowed and cold fingers seemed to clutch at his heart as he walked through that place of horror, picking his way between twisted and mangled bodies. Men and women, little children, babies even—the heart of a great city suddenly stilled in a pulse-beat. His blood chilled in his veins as those still faces stared up at him with unseeing eyes. He wanted to turn

away, to rush away from too much horror. But he had to look, had to stare down into the face of every dead woman as he approached the Times Building. He had to steel himself until he stood over the huddled heap that was Harriet Loomis and Evelyn Harvey.

Harriet, who was to have been a perfect wife for Phil Dawson.... Evelyn, the jolly companion whom he sometimes had thought that he, too, might ask....

The terrible blast had hurled them across Forty-second Street, had dumped them in the gutter amidst a litter of other corpses. Ralph Kennedy knelt beside them and stared into their dead faces with misted eyes.

What fiend out of the pit of hell could have perpetrated such a ghastly outrage? That question pounded in his brain, for he remembered the gloating faces of those killers who had murdered Phil Dawson. He knew that this was no frightful accident. Yet what was the meaning of this wanton slaughter—what was to be gained by it?

Kennedy didn't know, but his jaws clenched so tightly that his teeth hurt, and his hands balled into hard, white-knuckled fists. Grimly he vowed, in the presence of those innocent dead, that their murder would not go unavenged. Somewhere, someday, he would meet that thin-featured, vulpine face again....

IT WAS not until hours afterward that he learned the incredible magnitude of that frightful catastrophe. The explosion, for which there was not the slightest explanation, had occurred at Forty-fourth Street and Broadway, and for an eighth of a mile in every direction from that point it had spread instant death. A circle of death a full quarter-mile in diameter!

The toll of the dead ran into the thousands. Thousands of unsuspecting victims caught on the streets, in cars, in busses, in the subway below the street, in buildings facing the explosion. Not just those that were singled out for death by flying pieces of shot or shell—but everyone who came unprotected within its range. It was almost as if they had been stricken by gas poisoning, but the doctors denied that and definitely ascribed the deaths to shock—the fearful concussion of the explosion.

Hundreds of conflicting and often obviously imaginary stories from witnesses and supposed witnesses were published the next day, and in all of them there was no slightest worthwhile clue as to how the outrage had been perpetrated or why. Nor was there any mention of the three jubilant watchers who had shot down Phil Dawson.

Apparently Kennedy was the only one who had seen them, which probably accounted for the savagery with which he had been pursued. What he had seen was important—so important, he was convinced, that there was only one man in America to whom he would tell his story.

That man his fellow citizens knew as Operator 5, chief of the American Secret Service, the undercover ace to whom the nation was indebted for not only its freedom but its very existence.

Ralph Kennedy knew the amazing exploits of Operator 5,

as every man in America knew them. He knew how Jimmy Christopher had brought the country through the dark days of the Purple Empire, how he had rebuilt it from the ruins the Purple invaders left in their wake and how, since then, he had successfully defended it from the covetous grasp of scheming, power-hungry dictators. In his mind, Operator 5 had become a colossal figure—the one man who could combat this baffling and nation-threatening mystery.

Near stage fright threatened to overwhelm Kennedy when he reached Washington two nights after the Times Square outrage and arrived at the building which was Operator 5's headquarters. Nervously he glanced at his watch. Five minutes to eight—five minutes before his appointment with the undercover chief. The second floor, the telephone operator had told him. For a moment he hesitated, then decided to go upstairs and wait there.

Somebody was coming down from the second floor now, he noticed. A clean-cut, ruggedly capable-looking man, he made a mental note—and in that instant things started happening with lightning speed.

Suddenly a gun roared almost at his side—a gun from behind him, yet so close that he could see the flash and smell the burned powder. The man on the stairs hesitated in mid-step, seemed to back up, then bent over in the middle, slumped forward and came tumbling headlong, just as Kennedy whirled—and caught a glimpse of the same vulpine features that were stamped indelibly on his memory!

Just a fleeting half-glimpse, and then something came crashing down on his skull with terrible force. A blinding ball of fire exploded in front of his eyes, and he knew that he was falling....

CHAPTER 2
SEALED LIPS

JIMMY CHRISTOPHER was in his Washington office when news of the Times Square horror reached him. The regular weekly get-together of his "board of strategy," his most trusted and capable agents, had been held that evening, and now all had left but two of those who were closest to him.

Lithe, lean, wide-shouldered and narrow-hipped, he leaned back in his chair and swung away from the big desk with a map of the world beneath its glass top. Blue-eyed, sandy-haired, he seemed ridiculously youthful—preposterously so for a man of his accomplishments and responsibilities.

But in the lines of his clean-cut face was confidence and determination, the unmistakable stamp of authority that set him apart as a man born to command and lead his fellows.

"Even in these days of super-airships and stratosphere flying America should give daily thanks to the Almighty for the Atlantic and Pacific Oceans," he said thoughtfully. "How different our problem would be if we were connected to Europe, like Asia—or as close to it as Africa. Then we *would* have something to worry about, Tim."

Leaning over the desk, Tim Donovan was studying the big map with absorbed eyes. Those patches of color, each inhabited by another nation—another tribe of human beings ready to fly at the throat of their neighbors at the slightest provocation—never failed to fascinate him. Then his gray-blue eyes shifted from the map to the face of the man who was his idol.

Freckle-faced and pug-nosed, Tim Donovan was little more than a wiry youngster in his early twenties. But Jimmy Christopher counted it the luckiest day of his life when their trails had crossed. In those early days Tim had been a nondescript street urchin—a hungry, ragged bootblack shivering in a dark hallway in New York's slums. His quick warning had saved Operator 5 from an assassin's bullet—but that first service had since been dwarfed many times by the invaluable assistance he had rendered.

Between these two there had developed a remarkable trust, devotion and admiration that was mutual—a bond so close that Operator 5 placed more confidence in this stripling than in his most seasoned agents.

"But there's nothing to worry about now, Jimmy," Tim reiterated the conclusion the night's meeting had readied. "We are strong enough now so that nobody will try to jump us."

"And that is the time when our vigilance must be most untiring," came quietly from where a thin, gray-haired old man sat in an easy chair. "Don't forget, Tim, false security is the moment of greatest danger."

In those few words old John Christopher, the former Q-6 of American Intelligence, voiced the doctrine which he had bred into his son—the doctrine which had become Jimmy's creed.

"False security... the moment of greatest danger...." The familiar words were still echoing in his ears when the telephone rang and he lifted the receiver, to hear the excited voice of Gene Hornblow, his New York agent.

"Times Square... thousands killed... whole square blasted by a terrific explosion... no accident... no clue to the outrage... entire city in panic." Phrase after phrase impacted on his brain.

Months of peace and freedom from even the threat of war had given them a sense of security they had not enjoyed for years—and now this had come. What did it mean? The opening gun in a new attempt against America? The first warning that some hostile power thought the time ripe to leap at the throat of the lulled and unsuspecting republic?

"I am flying to New York immediately," he decided. "I'll take you with me, Tim. Dad, you will take charge here while we are gone. God knows what is behind such a barbarous outrage, but, whatever it is, we will nip it in the bud."

THAT WAS a laudable ambition, Jimmy Christopher admitted ruefully the next evening as he sat in a New York hotel room after a sleepless night and a long day of investigation that was dishearteningly fruitless. But no matter how he and his men had searched and questioned, there seemed not the slightest clue to be picked up. Nobody seemed to know what had set off the fatal blast. Nobody seemed to know from whence it had come.

All that he had to show for nearly twenty-four hours of work were several fragments of a peculiarly light metal which his men had discovered while combing the desolated square. Some of those fragments had been found embedded in the bricks of the buildings; some had been taken from the dead bodies of the victims. Parts of the bomb that had caused the explosion, undoubtedly—but that was about all he had been able to learn.

"This metal is lighter than aluminum, an alloy that is tough and yet almost weightless," the scientists to whom he rushed the specimens, reported. "If, as seems likely, these fragments were part of an aerial bomb, the metal probably was specially designed to release the explosive power with the slightest possible resistance."

That was when the telephone rang and John Christopher's voice, coming over the wire, added the final straw to a discouraging day.

"I do not know what you may have discovered, Jimmy," he said quietly, "but I can tell you that the Times Square explosion was no accident. There have been two more today. An explosion in the heart of Atlanta's business district at about six o'clock this evening took thousands of lives. Reports about that were still coming in when we had word from Chattanooga. You know they are holding a carnival celebration, and tonight was the grand finale parade. It was turned into a fearful slaughter when an explosion wiped out nearly all the marchers and the crowds that were watching."

New York, Atlanta and Chattanooga! Now there was no question that America faced a new and deadly peril—a peril that was the more dangerous because veiled in utter mystery. Baffled, groping helplessly in Stygian darkness, Jimmy did not know where to turn, how to attempt to fight—but he lost no time speeding back to Washington.

There the following day only added to his bewilderment and

growing apprehension. As in the case of New York, his best men were able to learn absolutely nothing in the Southern cities—and that evening Memphis joined the list of stricken cities when an explosion cleared out the waterfront just as a Mississippi River steamer was disembarking a capacity load of laughing and shouting excursionists.

"This is the work of a positive fiend!" Tight-lipped and hard-eyed, Jimmy put down the telephone after listening to the latest appalling bulletin from that horror-stunned town. "Diabolical murder—the cold-blooded slaughter of women and children! But what in God's name do the inhuman devils expect to gain by it?" He turned to where Gene Hornblow, come down from New York to report, sat beside his desk.

"Terrorism is the answer," Hornblow said grimly. "Just why, I am not sure—I have no definite lead, understand. But I do have a suspicion. A half-suspicion so nebulous that I do not feel justified in putting it into words—not until I have had a chance to investigate it more thoroughly. But if my hunch comes through, I'll have a report for you within the next twenty-four hours, Operator 5."

Jimmy tried to question him farther, but Hornblow was adamant in his refusal to go off half-cocked—and his chief knew him too well to try to press him. Hornblow was no alarmist. One of the most thorough men in the service, when he made a charge he would have the proof to back it up irrefutably. Until then, he would keep his mouth shut.

Jimmy watched his broad shoulders disappear through the doorway, then sat staring at the door panels abstractedly while

Hornblow's words ran through his mind. It was unusual for Gene to commit himself even that far until he had his case completely in hand—which must mean that he was pretty well convinced of his suspicions....

The bark of shots snapped Jimmy out of his preoccupation. A single shot... then two more. They were in the building—outside in the hallway!

Springing from his desk, he bolted from the room and hot-footed the length of the corridor. But when he reached the head of the stairway he saw that he was too late. The shooting was over, and two bodies lay huddled on the steps, one almost in the doorway.

Even before he reached the first still figure he knew what he would find. Gene Hornblow was lying on his face, but there was no mistaking those square shoulders. He was dead, the blood still trickling from the bullet hole that had been drilled through his heart. But even with that mortal wound, he had managed to cling to life until he had accounted for his killer. His automatic was still clutched in his relaxing fingers—and no more than ten feet from him lay the man he had downed, the murder gun just fallen from his nerveless hand.

A hard lump surged up into Jimmy's throat as he looked down at the face of the man with whom he had just been talking. Then he turned hard eyes to the murderer. Perhaps there would be something on the corpse to identify it—something that might point the way to the devils behind these bombing outrages. Already he was convinced that Hornblow had been shot down in order to stop his investigation of the Times Square outrage.

But when he bent over the fellow he found that the assassin was not yet dead. Blood gushed from two bullet holes in his chest. He was still breathing, although a slight moan ebbed from his lips. Staunching the flow of blood as well as he could, Jimmy propped up the wounded man on the stairs and hurried upstairs to summon an ambulance.

Half an hour later he stood beside the operating-table while a hospital surgeon probed the man's wounds and extracted two leaden slugs—two bullets that he knew, even before they went to the ballistics expert, had come from Gene Hornblow's automatic.

"If those bullets had gone half an inch lower he would be a dead man," the surgeon shook his head, "but he has a splendid heart and a husky young constitution. Chances are that he will pull through and be back on his feet in a few days. He ought to be conscious in an hour or less."

The wounded man was Ralph Kennedy, a resident of New York City, cards in his wallet revealed—and Jimmy Christopher's blue eyes took on the sheen of ice.

"I'll wait, Doctor—no matter how long it takes," he clipped, and then took up his vigil at the bedside.

IT WAS more than an hour before Ralph Kennedy was returned to consciousness and sufficiently in control of his faculties so that he could be questioned. During that interval, the slugs that had been taken from his chest had been to the ballistics expert who now had Gene Hornblow's weapon. They were returned with the report Jimmy expected. Gene's gun had fired them.

Kennedy must have read the grim accusation in Jimmy's eyes when the first question was plumped at him.

What was he doing there on the stairway when Hornblow was killed?

"I don't know what you think," the wounded man blurted suddenly, "but I had business there. I had an appointment." He looked around the room uneasily, as if he expected to find eavesdroppers spying on him. "An appointment with Operator 5."

"I am Operator 5." Jimmy's voice was brittle, the searching gaze of his cold eyes mercilessly probing.

"You... you...." Kennedy stammered in disbelief, and then seemed to realize his mistake. "I had an appointment with you," he exclaimed excitedly. "I didn't give my name. I just told the girl who answered the phone that I wanted to see you about the Times Square bombing. I was there, Operator 5—I saw it. I was just outside the death zone, and saw three men whom I am sure had something to do with it. That was what I wanted to tell you, why I came to Washington."

Nervously he related what he knew of the happenings in the hallway, and his fingers went to his head, probed gingerly where a patch of plaster had been affixed to his scalp. He seemed to be telling the truth, Jimmy admitted to himself. Yet the evidence against him was damning.

"So you had no gun?" Jimmy repeated. "And yet, when I found you, the weapon that killed Gene Hornblow was within a few inches of your hand—and we have found your fingerprints on the grip and the trigger! If there had been anyone behind you, Hornblow would have made no mistake. He never would have

put two bullets into you unless he was sure that you had fired on him. Your story isn't good enough."

"But I saw the killer," Kennedy protested desperately. "He was the same man I saw in New York, gloating over the Times Square bombing. The same man who chased me down the subway and tried to kill me."

"And tonight, when he had a chance to kill you, he killed Gene Hornblow instead and then ran off, trusting that a man who was already dead on his feet would finish you," Jimmy cut him short. "That doesn't make sense, Kennedy. You will be kept here under arrest until you are sufficiently recovered to remove you to a cell."

With that he turned his back on the expostulating patient, but before he left the hospital he had a quiet talk with the surgeon.

"That bump on his head—how do you suppose he got that, Doctor?" he questioned. "Hit his head on the steps when he went down, perhaps?"

"No, hardly that," the surgeon's brows lifted. "Such a blow would have inflicted a long, sharp cut. This was round and dulled, the scalp hardly torn—as if he had been hit with a blunted, padded weapon of some sort. Besides, from its position on his head, he would have to be a contortionist to have hit himself there while falling—practically would have had to stand on his head."

So, it appeared, that part of Ralph Kennedy's story might be true. Jimmy Christopher mulled over it as he left the building, tried to reconcile it with the rest of the evidence—and gradually a faint suspicion began to dawn in his mind, a plan began to form....

CHAPTER 3
EYES FROM THE SHADOWS

THE TELEPHONE was clamoring when Jimmy returned to his office, and intuition whispered its message even before he picked up the receiver. It was George Metcalf, up in Boston, who was on the line, although his shaky voice was hardly recognizable.

"We've had ours, Operator 5!" he gulped. "Ten minutes ago—on Boston Common. The Philharmonic concert was going on—one of the largest crowds of the season. Hell broke loose right in the middle of it. God only knows how many people were killed—it will run way up into the thousands. There must have been seven or eight thousand on the Common alone, and the dead were found for blocks on every side of it."

His voice broke, and Jimmy could hear him crying, struggling to fight back the sobs that choked him.

"God, it was frightful!" he gasped. "I never saw anything like that—even on the worst battlefields. Women and kids—all blown to pieces and piled up in heaps like raked-up rubbish!"

"How did it happen, George?" Jimmy at last managed to penetrate the near-hysteria that threatened to overwhelm the chattering Metcalf. "Give me some details. Are there any clues? Did you find anybody with worthwhile testimony?"

"Testimony—how could there be?" Metcalf half-groaned. "Anybody who saw what happened will never be able to testify in this world. Anybody who was within sight of the explosion was killed. There were two blasts, one a few seconds after the other. We've found the places where they landed, the craters they dug in the Common."

"Then you think they came from overhead?" Jimmy pressed.

"Can't see any other explanation." Metcalf had gotten hold of himself, was once more the keen, analytical secret service man. "The craters are not very deep, just a couple feet—remarkably shallow for an explosion of such terrific force. A buried mine would have made a far deeper excavation, and anything on top of the ground would have been seen—would have been bound to, where these went off."

There it was again... death had dropped from nowhere, apparently from out of the sky. Without warning and without leaving the slightest trace in its wake, it had swooped down and taken an appalling toll. Utterly wanton death that was seemingly without purpose....

Jimmy Christopher dropped the receiver back onto its hook and stared at it without seeing it. His blank eyes were looking far beyond the inanimate metal—were seeing the thousands of corpses that littered Boston Common, were seeing the mangled remains of victims in Times Square, in Atlanta, Chattanooga, Memphis. City after city, the dismaying death toll rising higher and higher—and still there was not a single clue to the method

He seized Diane's wrist.

or the meaning of these ruthless butcherings. Not a single lead—except this Ralph Kennedy.

Ralph Kennedy.... In that desperate moment Jimmy decided

to play the hunch that had been nagging him persistently. Quickly he reached for the telephone.

"Diane," he spoke into the receiver as soon as the soft, familiar "hello" came over the wire, "I have a job for you—nursing in the General Hospital. There is a case there who must be watched constantly, night and day. If you will tackle it, I think I can get Nan to come spell you."

"How soon, Jimmy?"

"Right away—if you can make it. There should be somebody there with him at this moment," he added apologetic explanation.

"I'll be ready as soon as I can put on a hat and coat and grab my over-night kit," came her answer, and Jimmy Christopher felt a warm glow well up in his heart.

Diane Elliot was his fiancée, but they were far more than sweethearts. They had been welded more closely together by unselfish service to their country than the marriage vows they would some day take could ever make them. Time and again they had faced death together, subordinating their love to the best interests of America. Their reward was a devotion from its citizens such as comes to few people in this world.

Ten minutes later Diane was at the office, ready to do whatever was expected of her. In the taxi that took them to the hospital Jimmy told her his suspicions and outlined his plan, and then for a moment the chestnut hair was very close to him as his lips clung briefly to hers.

"There should be no danger," he said thoughtfully, "but keep your eyes and ears open all the time. Let me know anything you may see or hear. You take the first stretch tonight, Di, and Nan will relieve you in the morning. I have already made all arrangements with the super."

A few words over the telephone had managed those details. When Diane arrived, a nurse was waiting to provide her with a uniform to lead her to the private room where Ralph Kennedy lay sleeping. After the nurse had gone, Diane walked over to the bed and looked down at the sleeper.

He seemed so young—her heart constricted as he moaned and tossed restlessly on his pillow. Half-intelligible sounds came from his lips, but she could make nothing of them.

After that he slept more quietly, and she went across the little room to the table and chair that were half-sheltered by a white screen. The minutes passed slowly; the hours dragged by. Eleven… twelve… one. Ralph Kennedy had not even awakened to ask for a drink.

IT WAS almost two o'clock before there was a break in the monotonous vigil. Then the door opened softly, and a white-clad orderly backed in, to hold the door aside for a wheel-table that another orderly pushed into the room. Diane came out from behind the screen and stepped to meet them before they could reach the bed.

"There must be some mistake," she said softly. "This patient is not to be moved under any circumstances. You must have the wrong room."

"This is two-seventeen, isn't it?" one of them asked. "That's the number we were given. No mistake about it. We're moving him up to four-thirty—that's a better room."

His partner nodded vigorous agreement, and they pushed past her toward the bed where the patient still slept.

Diane's eyes flashed angrily. "I tell you this patient is not to be moved," she insisted. "If you won't go back to the office, I'll call them."

Stepping back to her table, she picked up the telephone—and instantly the orderlies were after her. Leaping across the room, they upset the screen and grabbed the instrument out of her hands before she could say a word to the operator. Just in time to avoid their rush she sprang back, but they closed in on her from two sides, pushed her toward a corner.

Furiously she tried to fight them off, but now they were snarling and savage, all pretense dropped.

"Grab her before she can yell," the one who seemed to be the leader ordered. His own burly arms locked around her waist and slammed her back against the wall while his companion clamped a big hand over her mouth.

Diane felt his thick fingers at her throat, closing around her windpipe. Desperately she tried to scream, but one half-strangled cry was all that escaped from her lips.

That was sufficient.

Again the white door flung open, and through the doorway charged two grim-faced sturdy young huskies—Operator 5's men who had been stationed in the corridor as protection for Diane in case of trouble. With a curse one of the orderlies whirled and yanked a gun from beneath his coat.

But before he could press the trigger one of the undercover

men had reached him, was whipping an automatic barrel down over his skull.

The other white-clad masquerader was slower to realize his danger. His eyes widened with fear. Suddenly he threw Diane away from him and plowed straight into the antagonist who was leaping toward him, bowled him over with a head-on rush and dashed for the door.... But before he was half-way down the corridor he screamed once and then pitched on his face, a leaden slug buried in his brain.

In less than a minute it was all over, and the undercover men, assured that Diane was unharmed, were bending over the wounded man who lay beside Kennedy's bed. His skull was shattered, and blood was streaming down into his face, staining his white uniform a deep crimson. Diane took one look at him and sprang to the phone to call for a doctor. But she knew that there was nothing a physician could do for him. He was dying, out of his mind, muttering in delirium.

Not English words.... Was that French—or German? She listened closely and then recognized the half-German, half-French that is the *patois* of parts of Alsace-Lorraine. But his thoughts were rambling aimlessly, wandering back to the days of his childhood... and before the doctor arrived he was dead.

"An Alsatian," Jimmy Christopher wondered, when he had been summoned to the hospital, "and a recent immigrant, at that."

The dead man's papers had identified him as Louis Kreiter, a refugee from France. He had entered the United States only three months ago, with the assistance of Julius Schirmer, a highly respected New York financier and philanthropist who had been helping thousands of oppressed people to escape from the tyrants who now ruled their homelands.

The man who had been killed in the corridor carried nothing by which he could be identified but his face, unmistakably foreign, as were the pocket-knife, cigarette-lighter and fountain-pen his clothing yielded. Like his companion, he, too, evidently had been a recent arrival from Europe—and, like him, he probably also had fled from the tyranny of Evan Carliotti, who had overthrown the government of France to establish his own barbarous and autocratic rule.

Refugees helped from beneath the murderous heel of Carliotti, but almost as soon as they reached the shores of America they had turned on the host who welcomed them and become involved with this murderous campaign of wholesale bombing....

JIMMY WAS still mulling over the significance of that discovery the next morning when he reached his office. Oddly, he felt that the solution for which he was so frantically seeking was within reach of his hand. Tantalizingly, it eluded him because he could not read what should have been plain to him.

But hardly had he reached his desk than all thoughts of Kreiter and his companion were driven from his mind. Again the telephone demanded his attention—and over the wire came news that chilled his blood. Calamitous bulletins, one on the heels of the other.

Chicago was first, the staccato syllables of Walter Lochridge crackling over the wire like machine-gun fire.

"There's been hell to pay out here, Operator 5," he clipped. "Less than half an hour ago, when the streets were filled with people going to work. Half a dozen terrific explosions have just about depopulated Michigan Boulevard. The same old story—nobody saw anything, nobody has the slightest idea how it happened. All we know is that death rained down on the boulevard for a distance of almost two miles. We can't even begin to estimate the dead. The streets are filled with them, and the stores and office buildings are as bad if not worse."

And then came Kansas City.

"I've been trying to reach you since seven o'clock, Operator 5," the voice of Roy Hodges joined the chorus of disaster. "Things are in such bad shape out here that it's almost impossible to get a wire out of the city. We were bombed this morning—just about dawn. That's when the markets are crowded to capacity. There were two explosions, and they just about wiped out the whole lower end of the city."

"You have no idea how it happened? Nobody who witnessed it and can tell a coherent story?" Jimmy asked desperately.

"Not a thing," Hodges growled. "Anyone who witnessed it is piled up with the mounds of corpses we are still collecting. All we know is that two explosions were heard."

Death from nowhere! Death out of the empty air! Twice more it had rained down upon the earth and taken its appalling toll—

and not a soul could tell from whence it came! That seemed impossible. Surely there must have been someone who had seen the aerial bombs drop—if this slaughter was the result of aerial bombs. Surely someone must have seen the aircraft from which they dropped—if it was an airship that was the solution to that ghastly death-sewing.

All morning Jimmy sat at his desk and talked into the telephone—to his agents, police chiefs, newspaper editors, army officers and experts on explosives. But the answer was always the same—nobody knew *anything*.

Not a single clue... until New Orleans joined the ever-lengthening list of stricken cities.

It was midday, just after noon, that death came plummeting down into the center of the gulf port's wide Canal Street. Just after twelve o'clock, when the sidewalks were thronged with the lunch-hour crowd, two terrific detonations rocked the city and cleared the busy street like a freshly sharpened scythe sweeping through a stand of wheat.

One moment Canal Street was buzzing with life, echoing with talk and laughter punctuated by the insistent demand of automobile horns—the next a weird, hushed silence hung over it. A ghastly, funereal stillness that held interminably before the rush and scream of horrified spectators dashing into the awful shambles.

Even in the brightness of New Orleans' noonday, not a soul had seen the source of that fearful death scourge. Not a clue—until, later in the afternoon, when Luke Swazey discovered a

man who had been several blocks away from the scene of the disaster at the time of the explosion.

"He says he noticed something that struck him as peculiar, just a minute or so before the crash," Swazey telephoned to Operator 5. "The day was bright, with blinding sunshine and not a cloud in the sky. Yet he saw a big shadow pass over the street on which he was walking. Like a patch of cloud passing in front of the sun, only more sharply defined. But when he looked up there wasn't a thing in the sky, not a cloud anywhere."

"A shadow on the street, and nothing in the sky to produce it?" Jimmy mused. "That sounds pretty far-fetched."

"Yeah, sounds crazy to me," Swazey agreed promptly. "You know how it is, Operator 5. After something like this happens, people begin imagining they saw all sorts of things. This fellow says he didn't think much of it at the time, but after the explosion he remembered it and began to think maybe it was important. But that's the only thing we've been able to find that even faintly resembles a clue."

Three more cities pocked with death—and the only clue a man who *thought* he had seen a shadow on the street when the sky was empty and cloudless! For twenty minutes Jimmy Christopher sat at his desk while his brain labored mightily, his heart wrung with the agony of impotence. If there only was something to fight—but to sit there helplessly while thousands of innocent victims were cut down with impunity....

It was the anxious voice of President Andrew Warren that roused him from his near lethargy. Warren wanted to talk with him, wanted him to come to the White House for a consultation.

"Be there right away, sir," Jimmy answered automatically and reached for his hat—although he dreaded to face the harassed executive.

Andrew Warren took every one of these deaths as if the victim had been a member of his own family. He suffered with the bereaved relatives, almost dropped a tear on every newly made grave. Long days and sleepless nights he paced the floor of his study, vainly seeking the meaning of this implacable doom that hung over America. Imploringly he turned to Jimmy Christopher for aid, and Jimmy had failed him....

Bitterly Jimmy excoriated himself as the taxi sped him toward the Executive Mansion. Already he was facing Warren's haggard eyes, his worry-furrowed brow—when suddenly all the world seemed to rend apart in a terrific explosion! A crash so deafening that the sound of it stabbed into his ears like a white-hot bayonet!

Jimmy was only vaguely aware of what happened in that split-second. Thrown violently against one side of the cab, he felt the machine tip crazily on one side, saw the driver fighting desperately for control of the wheel. Then they were careening wildly, were rushing straight into the solid wall of a building—to meet it in a head-on crash.

The force of that collision snapped the door open, half-tore it from its hinges, and spilled Jimmy out onto the running-board. Stunned, his head whirling dizzily. He rolled into the street... but before he lost consciousness he glimpsed a shadow that momentarily enveloped the front of the big War Department Building. And yet in the same fraction of a second his eyes flashed upward, and he knew that the sky was *empty*—was perfectly clear in the strong beams of the setting sun!

CHAPTER 4
DOOM INVISIBLE

IT WAS three days before Jimmy Christopher was able to leave the hospital, but during that time he was far from idle. The moment he regained consciousness his brain began to spin and make plans. Lying on his cot, he spent long hours pondering this baffling death that came out of a clear sky. Gradually he forced himself to accept the explanation that must be the answer—no matter how incredible it might seem.

The Washington blast had taken its grim toll, had numbered some of the nation's leaders among its victims, but fortunately the White House had not been within the death radius.

"I almost wish that it had gotten me, Jimmy," President Warren sighed, as he sat beside the white bed. "Perhaps if I were gone the next administration might have more success fighting this baffling scourge. It marches on relentlessly—and we are making not the slightest progress in our attempts to cope with it. Not only Washington was bombed yesterday. Houston,

Texas, was almost wiped out by a deluge of death, and Minneapolis is still counting the dead. There was a state convention of the American Legion being held there... the slaughter was appalling."

Andrew Warren's handsome face was haggard from lack of sleep, his gray head bowed as if the weight of these holocausts was too much for him to bear. In his agonized eyes was the question that haunted him day and night.

"What can be behind this horrible campaign?" he again voiced the question he had asked a hundred times. "What can possibly be the motive for these atrocious outrages, Jimmy? America is at peace with the world. We have no dispute or quarrel with any nation."

"Evan Carliotti...." Jimmy began, but the President shook his head.

"We have been over all that," he said wearily. "Carliotti did have ambitions for world domination, but he has failed completely. You drove him out of America, and Great Britain has overthrown his regime and gotten back onto her feet. He still clings to France, but the country is utterly ruined, pillaged and sacked until it has been bled white. He has squandered his loot, and now he has no resources for a new attack on the United States. It isn't Evan Carliotti, Jimmy—I feel certain of that."

His head shook. "To the north of France we have Reichsfuehrer Schnabel, in Berlin, threatening a conquest of all Europe—but he has no time for America at this stage of the game. He has all he can manage, rattling the sword above the heads of his neighbors and browbeating them into submission. And yet these outrages very obviously are part of a deliberate campaign—a campaign of ruthless terrorism—against the United States. If only the inhuman monsters behind it would show their hands or let us know whom and what we are fighting!"

"Perhaps we can force them to make that revelation," Jimmy said tightly, desperate, a plan taking shape in his mind. "We *will* force them out into the open," he muttered, "but first we must take precautions against further raids that undoubtedly will come. We must take precautions to protect you, sir."

President Warren waved that suggestion away with an impatient little gesture, but Jimmy was adamant, and that afternoon the chiefs of the army engineering staff sat with him while they planned a series of bomb-proof shelters that would dot the capital from end to end.

"These shelters will protect anyone who manages to get into them," one of the engineers conceded dubiously. "The trouble is that there is never any warning. Death swoops down out of nowhere before anyone has a chance to dive to even the nearest shelter."

"That will be taken care of also," Jimmy nodded. "We are going to combat these raids, not just evade them."

Before evening another group of experts gathered in his hospital room—technicians who represented the aviation brains of the American Army. Carefully they listened to his directions and gave hearty approval. When they left to carry out his orders, Jimmy felt that at last he was making some progress and was laying a foundation for fighting off this murderous menace.

But the only hope of success depended upon more than

that—depended upon nothing less than willing self-sacrifice. What he needed was a Squadron of Death, a corps of men to whom life meant nothing when, by yielding it, they might purchase the salvation of their country! For hours he listed the names of men of that caliber, and dispatched to them the telegram that was a call to the colors.

THE NEXT morning they began to arrive. From all parts of the United States the noses of their planes began to converge on Washington. A host of human eagles to whom fear was something at which to laugh, they came grinning into Operator 5's room. They left with the same grin on their faces, and with a glint of steely determination in their eyes.

"You know that Seattle and San Francisco have just been bombed with a frightful toll of human life; that Denver and Birmingham received their baptism of death yesterday," he told them. "For a week disaster has been sprinkling every corner of our nation, and there seems to be no way to combat it. But there is a way we can put a stop to it, a way *you* can put a stop to it—if you are willing to pay the price."

Carefully he outlined his suspicions, the reasons for them, and the desperate plan that had evolved from them.

"The answer, of course, is death—*your* death," he finished gravely. "There is no possibility of escape, as you see. But by your death you will save the lives of thousands of helpless women and children and will have a part in ending the most barbarous menace that ever has faced America. You have the qualifications we need for this task. I offer you the opportunity that thousands of others would be eager to grasp."

"Put me down there for Boston," Stanley Peters grinned, as he nodded to the big outline map spread on Jimmy's lap. "I'm only afraid the skunks won't pay us another visit after what they did to the Common."

"Write me down for Philadelphia." Fred Crosby was hopeful. "They haven't put our number up yet, so maybe we'll be next on the list."

"Guess I can handle Detroit all right," Guy Bellinger grunted, "but Dune McDonald will sure be sore as a boil if I don't let him in on it."

One by one, Operator 5 checked off the principal cities of the country, assigning them to the volunteers. By the end of the third day his map was dotted with cross-marks and almost filled with the names written beside them. Names that constituted a Roll of Honor, whether or not those who bore them ever were called upon to redeem the pledge given.

When he strode out of the hospital he felt at last ready to pick up the bloody gauntlet these skulking murderers had thrown into the face of America.

From the hospital Jimmy went straight to the White House, where President Warren awaited him impatiently in his study.

"Thank God, you're on your feet again, Jimmy!" the Chief Executive greeted. "We can't afford to lose you now. That was a close call you—and America—had." Then his eyes strayed to the littered top of his desk, and his shoulders slumped discouragedly. "You heard about Los Angeles last night—the mayor and more than three thousand people killed?"

"Yes, I heard," Jimmy said quietly. "Ed Wales was in to see me yesterday. He will take charge of the Los Angeles defense, but of course this happened before he had time to return to the coast. It is this defense plan I want to talk to you about."

For fifteen minutes he outlined the preparations he had made and explained how the system would operate. Listening, Andrew Warren's eyes grew wide with wonder and pride.

"God bless them!" he murmured softly. "It is a terrible thing that such a sacrifice should be necessary, but America is fortunate that in her hour of need she has men like this. To step into a plane and know that you are flying to certain death...."

His voice faded into a whisper as he visualized the magnitude of the deed these men were willing to perform. For a moment there was silence in the study—and then the stillness was shredded by the warning blast of a shrill, penetrating siren. Raucously it screamed notice that the constantly listening watchers, whom Operator 5 had posted around the city, had picked up the sound of an approaching plane with their delicate vibration-detecting instruments. Danger was swooping down on Washington!

"Downstairs in the bomb-proof, sir—that's where you belong," Jimmy snapped, and despite Warren's protests he rushed the President to the protection of the steel-and-concrete shelter that had been constructed beneath the White House.

FROM THE Executive Mansion Jimmy raced to a taxicab, sprang behind the wheel himself when the terrified driver deserted it and ran for the nearest air-raid refuge. At top speed he drove to the municipal flying field and arrived there just in time to see three planes taking to the air.

Leaping from the cab, he raced to another hangar and helped the fieldmen open the big doors.

"All right, Moriarity!" he shouted to a mechanic who came running toward him. "I'll take it up. Hop in and get the detector working!"

The planes, bursting into flame, filled the sky with human torches!

Moriarity sprang into the rear cockpit. Before the plane left the field he had a helmet-like arrangement over his head and was listening to the vibrations of a sensitive electric "ear" which

must serve them instead of eyes to pick out this oncoming invisible menace.

Straight for the White House the three planes speeded, and behind them Jimmy Christopher coaxed every possible ounce of speed out of his motor. Desperately he strove to overhaul them, to take the lead in this race in which death must be the reward of the winner. But those planes were as fast as the one he piloted, and their lead was too great.

They kept their distance, winging on there ahead of him—and then the one that led the trio banked and dived headlong. Before the others could follow, that dive stopped short. Amazingly the plane brought up short in mid-air—seemed to smash into something solid and pancake against it. Instantly there was a terrific crash, a blinding explosion—and like a great aerial bomb the entire plane disintegrated!

Jimmy Christopher's hard eyes narrowed, and his clenched lips trembled in a word of prayer for the fearless souls who sped into the jaws of death with that load of swift destruction.

For an instant he could see only the falling debris of the shattered plane, and then the very air seemed to break into flame. A great bonfire had kindled there in the heavens and now started to plummet earthward. With a crash that sent flames spewing in every direction, it struck—and then burst open on the ground!

Spiraling downward as swiftly as he dared, Jimmy landed

with great care a hundred yards from the blazing pile. Before he could scramble out of the cockpit another explosion shook the earth and the roaring bonfire flew in every direction. One of the soaring patches of flame landed less than ten feet from him, and instantly he leaped upon it, trampling it and beating it out with his flying helmet.

At last the flames were extinguished, and he stooped to pick up a patch of the siding of airplane fuselage. One side of that patch was blackened by fire—but, when he turned it over, the other unharmed side was almost invisible to the naked eye!

Now, out of that blazing inferno that filled the street from side to side, the blackened metal skeleton of a huge airship began to materialize—and Jimmy at last had solved the mystery of the invisible doom that had been terrifying the nation! As he had suspected, those terrible aerial bombs were dropped by airplanes which had been rendered invisible by some sort of treatment or preparation entirely unknown to American scientists.

And with this vindication of the hunch on which he had based his combat plans, he knew that he had ended the dread scourge.

In scores of other cities flying martyrs were at that moment stationed near their explosive-laden planes, waiting for the word to take to the air—and die. Hundreds of watchers were listening intently for the telltale vibration of an airplane motor. The moment the approach of the unseen raiders was detected, those flying torpedoes, guided to their mark by the back-seat listeners, would be hurled at the invisible menace.

A head-on collision was the only way in which that menace

could be met, and such Spartan tactics meant the end of the death-rainers. The bombing campaign was thwarted; and now, if Dr. Norman King and the scientists he had gathered around him could discover the nature of the preparation that gave this weird quality of invisibility—if they could devise a way of overcoming it—the last vestige of the peril that had baffled the entire country would be removed....

FILLED WITH triumphant elation, Jimmy hurried to the government research laboratories, especially organized and equipped for work of this sort, with the specimen he had salvaged.

Dr. King studied the strip of fuselage and whistled softly. "Damnedest thing I ever saw," he muttered. "I wonder if there is any possible connection between this and what happened to Governor Calhoun a little while ago in Frankfort."

"Governor Calhoun.... Frankfort?" Jimmy echoed his words.

"There was an Associated Press flash about it on the radio a few minutes ago," King explained. "The Kentucky governor was addressing a great gathering at the state fair in Frankfort this afternoon when suddenly he and all those on the speakers' platform with him were wiped out. They seemed to melt away into nothingness as the stand disintegrated with them before the astonished eyes of the crowd."

He went on, "At first the listeners thought it was some sort of trick. They laughed and waited for the platform to reappear—until someone walked through where the platform had stood and found nothing but emptiness—a few heaps of dust on the ground. Then they began to realize that they had actually seen a dozen men vanish, apparently swallowed up into nothingness. Blind panic seized them and hundreds were tramped in the stampede to escape."

Now he frowned. "It is remotely possible that the stuff which makes this piece of fuselage almost invisible might have been used in some way to spirit the men away. But how they could have gotten rid of a solidly built speakers' platform is more than I can figure!"

But Jimmy Christopher hardly heard what he was saying. In a moment all his elation had ebbed from him, and once more a blank wall of eerie, baffling mystery rose mockingly before his eyes....

CHAPTER 5
DANGER CALLING—FOR AMERICA!

ROUGH HANDS grabbing his covers awoke Ralph Kennedy from a coma-like sleep. For a moment the little hospital room seemed to be filled with wraithlike figures that whirled and danced around him. Then his feverish eyes began to clear, focus, and an inkling of what was transpiring began to penetrate his understanding.

But for the intervention of the guards from the hallway he would have been kidnaped. The only one who could have any reason for kidnaping him was the vulpine-featured individual responsible for his present predicament. Not satisfied with having him under arrest, facing a term in prison if not a death sentence, this fellow and his mates seemed determined to eliminate permanently the one man who could identify them. That was the reason for their relentless hounding.

Kennedy's blood ran hot in his veins and a flash of rage-kindled fever bathed his body with perspiration. Once more he solemnly vowed to avenge himself upon the devils who had murdered Phil Dawson and the Loomis and Harvey girls....

Kennedy made his plans carefully, watching his chance. It came at last. His day nurse, Miss Elliot, stepped out of the room—and instantly he went into action. Getting out of bed, he ran to the open window and pushed the sash higher. He raised one leg to the sill, began to boost himself—then suddenly catapulted his body backward with all his strength.

He dived straight at the guard who came running to stop him. His arms closed around the man's knees, swept him off his feet and bore him backward. The guard's head hit the floor with a bang—and he rolled limply on one side. For a moment Kennedy clung to him, but there was no more fight in the fellow. That thump had knocked him out.

Quickly Kennedy stripped off the guard's clothing and put them on himself. With an automatic gripped ready in the pocket of his newly acquired coat, he tiptoed cautiously to the door, inched it open. The corridor was deserted. With a fine show of confidence he stepped out into the hallway and walked to the stairs.

Half a dozen nurses and orderlies he passed, but they gave him not even a second glance. Without interruption he went through the reception hall and down the broad steps. Free at last! His pulses beat fast as he filled his lungs with the cool air of early dusk and strode down the street.

Tensely he listened. At any moment he expected to hear a clamor behind him, but he reached the end of the hospital block and nothing had happened. Glancing back over his shoulder, he saw that nobody was pursuing him—saw, also, that a sedan was drawing up to the curb just beside him.

That car meant nothing to him for a moment—and then, when a swift warning flashed to his brain, it was too late. Two men had sprung out of it, and before he could suspect their intention they were upon him, had seized him, pinned his arms at his side, and dragged him through the doorway. The cold, hard muzzles of automatics ground into his neck and into his ribs, and the weapon he clutched was wrested from his fingers before he could get it out of his pocket.

Helpless, he lay panting on the back seat as the sedan sped across Washington, past the public buildings and into the poorest section of the city. There it came to a stop in front of a dilapidated three-story wooden structure. For a moment his captors glanced up and down the shabby street to see that the way was clear. Then he was rushed across the sidewalk and into a street-level door that opened when they reached it.

The sound of that door closing behind him rang in Kennedy's ears like the clap of doom—and the moment he faced the man who confronted him inside the building he knew that his fears were fully justified. In a barely furnished room at the rear of the second floor he was marched into the presence of his vulpine-faced nemesis.

"So Operator 5's bright young assistant has decided to pay us a visit!" he sneered, and his mean little eyes glittered malignantly. "That being the case, you may want to answer a few questions—just so that we get along more pleasantly together. First of all, I want to know how you happened to be on hand to spy on us the night of the Times Square party. I want to know what you reported to Operator 5. I want to know how much he thinks he knows about recent occurrences that have somewhat startled this country. Speak up, fellow—I have no time to waste!"

The suave, gently mocking voice hardened, ending like the snap of a whip. As it echoed in his brain, Kennedy thought quickly. These fellows evidently thought he was one of Operator 5's staff—thought that he had been stationed there on Broadway deliberately the night of the accident. They were worried about what Operator 5 might know—and he wanted to keep them worried. Grimly he clenched his jaws and glared his defiance.

"So you won't talk?" the silky voice struck at him like a rattlesnake. "Perhaps we can convince you that it is wiser to be more sociable. Take care of him," he nodded to his assistants.

THERE WERE four of them in the room—the two who had brought Kennedy and two already on hand when he arrived. Instantly they grabbed their prisoner and wrestled him out of his coat, tore open his vest and shirt. The wounds in his chest were still heavily bandaged. Callously they seized the gauze wrappings and ripped off, plucked the dressings from the partially healed wounds.

Brutally one of the fellows jabbed his thumb against the

bullet-torn flesh and ground it in mercilessly—again and again, until blood gushed from the freshly inflamed wound.

"Oh-oh!" the vulpine face chided mockingly. "You have been too rough with him. Better cauterize that wound."

Grinning evilly, another of the gang, who had just lit a big cigar, stepped forward and puffed until the coal gleamed with fire—and in that sickening moment Ralph Kennedy realized the ordeal that awaited him. Resolutely he locked his teeth together and steeled himself for the torture that was coming... but it was even worse than he anticipated. It was unendurable—pure, unmitigated hell as that gleaming coal bored into the quivering flesh like a red-hot poker.

"Now does your tongue feel any looser?" the silky, mocking voice cut through his agony.

Kennedy could feel the perspiration oozing out on his forehead in great beads, then streams that trickled down his face. But not a sound escaped from his lips. How long he could stand this agony he did not know, but he would endure it until he collapsed. That, he told himself half-deliriously, was the least he could do to fight these devils who had slaughtered thousands of innocent victims—the least he could do for Phil and Harriet and Evelyn.

Again that brutal thumb was boring into him, tearing away the half-mended tissue. Again blood spurted and that terrible cigar came closer... but before it could reach Kennedy's cringing flesh the open doorway of the room seemed to spew forth a horde of men. Actually there were only five of them—five young men scarcely out of their teens—but they swept in like an army and flung themselves upon the kidnapers.

Instantly the small room became a bedlam. Shots and the thud of blows mingled with curses and groans, with screams that ended in choked gurgling. Kennedy saw two of those inhuman devils topple to the floor, another was shot down as he tried to reach the doorway.

Now the relentless avengers closed in on the two survivors—Vulpine Face and one other.

IN THE lead of the attackers dashed a small, wiry stripling with a freckled face and pug nose—a youth whom Kennedy did not know, could not identify as Tim Donovan. Unknown to him, Tim and his four young companions—whom Operator five had appointed as his junior auxiliary—had been on guard outside the hospital, watching from a safe covert, ever since an undercover man had reported a suspicious-acting car lurking in a side street beside the building.

That was several days ago, and since that time Operator 5's plan had been made. It had been waiting to be put into execution only until Kennedy was sufficiently recovered to leave the hospital. Quite unknown to the bed-ridden patient, Kennedy's improvement had been carefully noted. The desperate plans formulating in his brain had been read almost as clearly as if printed on his forehead. The opportunity to escape, upon which he had seized so eagerly, had been deliberately prepared for him on Jimmy Christopher's orders.

But Jimmy had not counted on the bestiality of these inhuman monsters, or foreseen the ordeal Kennedy had had to endure. It had taken time for Tim and his companions to break into the building... and what they beheld when they charged into the torture room only added to their fury.

Savagely Tim hurled himself at the sharp-faced individual whom he identified as the leader of the outfit. But one of the wounded men on the floor writhed into his path and almost sent Tim headlong. That near tumble saved his life, for Vulpine Face triggered an automatic at him at point-blank range. Tim felt the bullet cut past his ear—then was at grips with the other survivor, whipping down at him with an automatic barrel.

That took a split-second—all the time the mean-eyed leader needed. Springing to one side of the room, he flung himself into a heavy chair that stood against the wall, grasped its arms with his hands—and the chair turned over backward. With it went a section of the floor beneath and a panel of the wall at its rear. Like one of the compartments of a paddle-wheel, the whole thing turned over noiselessly... and into place slid another section of floor and wall that clicked metallically as they closed.

At the same instant the one door that opened into the room swung shut, and again, the metallic click gave an ominous hint of the solidity of the barrier.

Momentarily Tim stood there spellbound, gaping at the spot where a second before the chair had stood. Then he flung himself at the wall, put all his strength against it, stamped on the floor. But both were unyielding. Both fitted so closely that the seam of their joint with the rest of the room was barely discernible. The door, too, fitted so precisely that he surmised that the room was air-tight.

The place was a deadly trap. A gas chamber? Perhaps. Or if not that, a room where they could be left to starve to death if they did not smother when the supply of oxygen was exhausted.

Tim's face was paler than usual when he turned to his companions, but before he could speak a jeering voice mocked at him from a slit that opened in one of the walls near the ceiling.

"Nice and tight, isn't it?" the triumphant leader chuckled. "Those walls are solid steel, if you have not made that interesting discovery already. You would need a fieldpiece to batter your way out, so you might as well save your hands. Might as well sit down and make yourselves comfortable—or at least as comfortable as you can expect to be inside an oven. You are going to roast, my friends. Listen to this—do you know what it is?"

Through the slit came the unmistakable sound of striking matches and then the crackle of flames!

"That's right—fire," the taunting voice jeered. "This old shack is a tinderbox, but I am setting it off so that the inside will be a bonfire before the flames reach the street and attract attention. A fine big bonfire, with you roasting to a crisp in the middle!"

Tim triggered a shot at the narrow slit, but he heard the bullet slap harmlessly against solid metal. The taunting ended in a mocking laugh, and now the opening was gone.

White-faced but unafraid, Tim Donovan and the others in that fiendish trap looked Death in the face....

HIS SHARP-FEATURED face twisted and twitching with hatred, Kennedy's nemesis applied his matches with diabolical cunning. Then, his task finished, he started for the front door and the sedan that stood at the curb. But before he reached the door it opened and a woman ran from it to the car, stepped into the rear and crouched low on the floor, a lap-robe drawn over her.

The incendiary did not see her. Nor did he see the other shadowy figure that hid away in the closet of a room on the first floor of the doomed building. With evil satisfaction he locked the door behind him. But the moment the lock clicked that closet door opened, and out stepped a girl whose features bore a remarkable similarity to those of Jimmy Christopher.

Nan and Jimmy Christopher were twins, but her blond hair, full red lips and bright blue eyes, added just the needed touch of charming femininity to add beauty to the clean-cut features with which they were both endowed. Now her face was pale and tense, the smoke fumes in her nostrils sending little shivers of panicky fear through her. But she resolutely mastered her trepidation.

Running upstairs, she hurried to the room where Tim and his companions were locked. The door was fast, although she could see no sign of a lock. It did not even tremble when she lunged at it with all her strength. Solid steel, it seemed to be—and with a sinking heart she realized that even a fire-ax would be useless against it. Nothing but high-power explosives would batter that door in. By the time she could secure anything of that sort and return with it to the building, the place would be in ashes.

Already she could hear the crackle of flames all around her, and the billowing smoke was becoming thicker. But there must be *some* way of getting into that room! Frantically she circled it, pounding against the walls, listening for a hidden panel, for a point of weakness.

There seemed to be none whatever, and now the heat that came up from the lower floor was almost overpowering. The fires had been craftily lighted so that the floor beneath that prison room was blazing fiercely. The rooms connecting with it on three sides were rapidly becoming raging infernos.

Nan coughed and gasped for breath. The smoke clutched at her throat, blurred her eyes, made her dizzy and faint. But she persisted in a task that her common sense told her was hopeless. Pounding, testing, going over every square foot of the walls—she finally reeled and fell to the floor. Groggily she got back onto her knees, put her hands against the wall for support… and then an amazing thing happened right beside her.

A part of the wall and floor gave way noiselessly, flapped through the air like big wings. The wall section swung down and became part of the floor. A new section moved into place in the wall—and in another moment it was as if she must have dreamed what she had seen!

Nan knelt there beside the wall. Carefully she kept her hands in place, pressed again. Once more the paddle-wheel miracle occurred before her eyes—but this time the wall section that moved outward had a chair attached to it. In that chair sat Ralph Kennedy, her late patient at the hospital!

"They made me come first," Kennedy gasped, as he spilled out onto the floor and sank to his knees beside her. "Thank God, you found out how this thing operates. We were almost stifled!"

Again she pressed the wall, and the sections operated soundlessly.

"It takes two revolutions to bring the chair out," Kennedy told her. "The devil who thought this out missed nothing. The arms of the chair operate the mechanism from the inside. But once it is used to make an escape it does not return to the room unless this outside arrangement is used to send it there."

One after the other, the red-faced, perspiration-drenched youths emerged from the oven that had so nearly snuffed out their lives. Last of all came Tim Donovan. He was barely in time, for now a solid blast of flame was roaring up the stair-well and the building had become untenable.

Rushing to the front of the house, the men smashed open one of the shuttered windows and leaped down to the street.

"You sure came in the nick of time, Nan," Tim panted when they had carefully lowered their savior to safety. "But where is Di—she was on day duty at the hospital, wasn't she?"

"Yes," Nan Christopher said softly. "We came here together, but she insisted that I stay and see that you got out safely. She went off with the fiend who set this fire. God only knows what has happened to her by now! Alone against a monster like that!"

BUT DIANE ELLIOT was not counting the odds against her at that moment. Crouched in the back of the speeding car, she was doing her best to keep track of where it was they were going. Desperate plans for overpowering the man at the wheel rushed through her brain. It could not be now but perhaps later—when he had arrived at his destination. Before he had time to leave the car she must spring up and get the drop on him, must tie him up....

In the midst of that planning, the car suddenly swerved off

the highway and in under a brightly lighted gas station portico. Barely in time she sank flat on the floor and clutched her automatic, ready for instant action if he should open one of the rear doors.

But that emergency passed. Refueled, the car turned back onto the road without the driver having even left his seat. On into the gathering dusk it sped, and Diane cautiously raised herself, lifting her head as they dashed through a small town and passed its railroad station. There should be a name over this station. There was—but before she could make it out, disaster overwhelmed her.

With a sudden swerve the driver swung into an empty parking-lot, jammed on the brakes—and flung himself over the seat! Right on top of her he landed, bearing her to the floor and grabbing her through the hampering lap robe. Diane fought desperately, but his sudden attack had stunned her, knocked the breath from her lungs. Before she could use her gun her wrist was on the floor beneath his knee, was being ground cruelly as he wrested the weapon from her fingers.

"Now perhaps we are better able to understand each other," he growled. "It would be inadvisable for you to scream. That would compel me to hit you with this gun—very hard, over the head or in the face. That would not be pleasant. You are going to lie very still while I tie you up so that you don't get into trouble."

There was something familiar about that voice—something hauntingly familiar about the half-glimpses she had caught of his face. Now she got a good look at him—and recognition dawned.

"You... why, you are Henry Gerber... Julius Schirmer's secretary!" she accused. "I remember you were with him at Governor Wiley's inauguration reception last January. I met you—"

"And I remember you, my dear Miss Elliot," Gerber assured her suavely, cold steel beneath his unctuous tones. "It is somewhat unfortunate that you recognized me—for, of course, that dooms you. But, since you are Diane Elliot, I do not believe I shall slit your throat just yet. You have a bit longer to live—and some very interesting things to see."

As he spoke, he took a length of stout rope from a pocket of the car and lashed her arms at her sides, then tied up her feet. Lastly he forced a folded towel between her jaws and fastened it securely there. Trussed and helpless, she lay on the floor, glaring her defiance and contempt. But Henry Gerber chuckled with satisfaction as he returned to his place behind the wheel.

Once more the car started off and sped into the night that was closing in upon it Diane Elliot marveled at the astonishing development that had transformed the young socialite secretary to one of New York's best known millionaires into a fiendish killer, who spoke of death as if it were no more than a routine engagement he was making for Julius Schirmer....

CHAPTER 6
THE ROAD TO HELL

RUTH DARROW sat in her brother's coupé and hardly saw the road along which they were driving. That road led to Canondale, led home—and the thought filled her heart with a delicious warmth. Home.... A year ago it had seemed that her home must be broken up. That was when Dr. Eli Darrow had been stricken with a mysterious and apparently unknown malady. Illness of that sort is costly. The dollars had flowed away like water, and Dr. Darrow had seemed to get no better—not until they took him to the expensive Milo Clinic in Columbus six months ago. There his improvement started almost at once—slow, of course, but steady.

That, too, had taken money. All that she could earn by teaching school, and all that Jeff, the big husky at the wheel, could make by working sixteen hours a day in his garage. But this day had been worth it—well worth all the months of working and scrimping!

A tender smile flitted over Ruth's handsome, intelligent face, and her arm tightened around the shoulders of the old man who sat between her and her brother. Dr. Darrow had made a complete recovery. Today he was going home—and now the smile on his daughter's delicate features was secure.

Doctors are important people in a little town of twenty-five hundred souls—especially when they are patient, kindly, hard-working practitioners like Dr. Eli Darrow. Their neighbors and fellow-townsmen esteem them highly—much more highly than the benevolent old physician had any idea. But today he was going to learn the depth of that affection.

That was the surprise she and Jeff were keeping from him. Dr. Darrow knew that he was going home, but had no suspicion of the changes he would find in the little Southeastern Ohio town. He had no suspicion of the uniformed band that was waiting to receive him at the edge of Canondale, of the gay decorations that outdid anything the town had ever achieved, of the hundreds of neighbors massed at his home, waiting to serenade him.

Ruth's lips quivered and tears welled up into her brown eyes. This would be a homecoming and testimonial such as Canondale had never seen. Her heart fluttered excitedly and a thrill of anticipation trickled down her spine as they rounded the last turn in the road. Now there remained less than a quarter of a mile. There, just ahead, was Orrin Dillman's big farmhouse close to the road.... But suddenly she blinked unbelievingly. Orrin Dillman's house *had* been there. It had *always* been there... *but now it wasn't!* It had vanished!

For one horrible moment Ruth Darrow thought that she was going blind. Canondale, just coming into view in the distance, had vanished with the Dillman house—had vanished with all the rest of the world! Now Jeff was jamming his foot down on the brake, was staring through the windshield with bulging eyes and sagging jaw as he brought the car to a stop no more than twenty feet from where the road ceased to be—*twenty feet from where the whole world apparently ceased to be!*

"God A'mighty!" gasped from Jeff Darrow's blanched lips, but his sister was mute. She could only sit there and stare as if turned into a statue.

Out there in front of them was only a vast desert waste—a waste that had been created before her eyes, even though the very idea of what she had witnessed bore the taint of madness!

Ruth Darrow had seen houses, trees, fences, even the road itself, disintegrate and melt away into nothing! Everyday commonplaces that she had known and seen every day of her life. Where they had been now there was nothing but little mounds and ripples of dust and sand! Canondale and all the surrounding territory had vanished as if the whole scene had been merely a tantalizing mirage!

Incredulously the three Darrows sat there and stared into that desolate waste. After that first involuntary exclamation from Jeff, not a word passed their lips—for this was a thing that dwarfed the capacity of words. Transfixed, they sat there and scarcely breathed... until they saw something that seemed to be moving out there in the new-made wilderness. Nothing tangible, nothing real—and yet there seemed to be a wraith-like stirring out there in the dust. Ruth blinked her eyes to be certain that this was not another mirage. But there was *something* coming toward them. Apparently nothing more than little puffs of dust stirred up by the breeze—but from them came the bark of a shot, the typewriter-like clatter of a machine-gun!

JEFF DARROW snapped to his senses with a start as suddenly the windshield in front of him was lined with bullet-stars. While bullets rattled against the car, he bent over the wheel swung the coupé in a circle and headed back in the direction from which they had come.

One hand clutching the side of the door, the other fastened tight on her father's shoulder, Ruth did not draw a breath until the maneuver was completed and they were speeding away from that incredible waste. Looking back through the rear window, she saw that the dust puffs followed them right up to the road—and still came after them over the hard concrete!

"Faster, Jeff—*faster!*" she begged. "They're com—"

Suddenly the rear window dissolved into shattered fragments. Ruth ducked to one side to escape the shower of flying glass, tried to pull her father to safety—and realized, with a surge of horrible fear, that he had slumped in her arms.

"Daddy... *Daddy!*" she screamed wildly, as she shook the limp figure. "Speak to me! You've *got* to speak to me!"

Then her eyes fastened on the bloody horror the bullets had made of the back of his skull. A great sob was torn from her—a sob that was only a faint echo of the excruciating pain that stabbed into her heart. He was dead... poor, inoffensive Dr. Eli, who had never harmed a soul, shamefully murdered just when he had won a new lease on life.

"He's dead, Jeff," she half-whispered to her brother, but she could hardly believe the import of what she said.

Alive a moment ago, and now dead—murdered by *nothing!* By a dust cloud that came puffing out of the desert wilderness where Canondale should have been! It was fantastic—utterly mad! The whole thing was preposterous, the wild concoction of an insane mind!

That was it—she was mad! Stark mad! There was nothing the matter with her father. He was sitting there quietly, saying not a word because he knew that she was mad. That was why Jeff had turned the car. He did not dare take her to Canondale; instead, he was speeding her to an asylum. That was why he looked so ghastly, so utterly terrified. He had seen her go mad and did not know what she would do next....

Ruth caught herself just in time. Resolutely she checked her hysteria before it did drive her over the brink into insanity. Dr. Eli *was* dead, and with his death something had died within her own breast—something that now gave way to a grim, implacable determination, an avid, bitter thirst for revenge against heaven only knew whom or what....

Jeff Darrow drove as if the devil himself were pursuing the car. Wildly he sped onward, with never as much as a glance over his shoulder. Through village after village, and still that mad speed did not diminish. There was little traffic in this part of the country—hardly any until they approached Parkersburg, just over the border in West Virginia.

This was where a state trooper sirened up beside them and raced his motorcycle at their running-board for several miles before Jeff finally slackened speed and then came to a stop. "Seventy-five—nearly eighty!" the outraged officer fumed. "What do you think this highway is—a racetrack? What do you—"

Then he saw the dead man in Ruth's arms, and his eyes widened.

"What's this? How'd that happen? Where you going with that man?" Questions popped from him, but Jeff hardly seemed to hear.

"Back there—where Canondale ought to be," Jeff said tonelessly. "There's nothing there now but a desert—miles and miles of desert and little puffs of dust that sweep up on you. They did *that* to him. They killed him. They're chasing us. They'll be here any minute now—and then they'll kill us all."

"Puffs of dust killed him—and did that to your windshield,

I suppose?" the trooper demanded with elaborate sarcasm. But when the girl nodded and seriously corroborated that crazy yarn his eyes became like saucers. He tried to sniff surreptitiously.

Drunk—or crazy? He didn't know which, but certainly this was a case of one or the other. But how their car got in such a condition....

"This is nothing, officer," the girl was saying. "Just one man. There are hundreds—thousands—who must have died back there, where Canondale used to be. But there is nothing you can do. There's nothing there anymore, *nothing*—"

"I don't know anything about that." The trooper took determined charge of that madhouse situation. "But if that man was murdered on the road near Canondale, I want to know more about it. We're going back there. Turn your car. I'll ride beside you."

Back along that road to hell they drove, Jeff an automaton at the wheel and Ruth staring stonily ahead of her—back to the end of everything. But when they approached the jumping-off place they saw that a score of cars were parked at the limit of the bleak wilderness. A crowd of nearly a hundred people had gotten out to walk to the edge of the desolation.

Open-mouthed they stood and gaped at that astounding scene. Then they shuffled uneasily, their eyes sought one another's—and they slunk away as the chill fear of the unknown, of eerie, unaccountable doom, seeped into their stunned brains and stole the courage from their hearts.

"What in hell..." the trooper began, as soon as he got off his motorcycle, but when he looked out over that weird waste the bluster went out of him. "Where—where is Canondale?" he asked of nobody in particular. "This road—what happened to it?"

Squatting at the end of the solid highway, he ran his fingers through what had been concrete, and through them sifted a powdery dust that was even finer than the cement from which the concrete had been made. Gingerly he stepped out into it, trusted his weight on it experimentally, and then waded through dust that was nearly six inches deep—dust that rose up and choked him as his footsteps stirred it up....

TEN MINUTES later the unbelievable news of that blasted wilderness that had suddenly blotted out a prosperous community was on the telegraph wires, speeding to every part of the Union. It reached Operator 5 at Frankfort, Kentucky, where he was vainly trying to discover what had happened to Governor Calhoun and the committeemen who had been with him on the speakers' stand when it disappeared from the face of the earth. Not the slightest trace had been found of the governor or any of his companions since they had vanished into empty air before thousands of astonished onlookers. With the grandstand on which they had been seated, they seemed to have completely evaporated.

The police had roped off the space in which the grandstand had stood, and Jimmy had gone over it carefully. He had fingered the powder-fine dust that lay in little heaps on the ground. He had examined the electric wires that supplied power for the amplifying system, had seen where they appeared to be sheered off cleanly where they approached the stand. He had found the feet of the structure's corner-posts still embedded in the earth—but that was all that remained of the stand and those who had occupied it.

Jimmy was dumfoundedly on the point of returning to Washington, when one of his men brought him word of the news flash. His eyes kindled.

"Layers of powder-fine dust," he repeated thoughtfully. "That is what we have here—apparently the only remains of Governor Calhoun and his associates. This Canondale mystery sounds like more of the same deviltry—perhaps the next step after a test of some terrible new weapon was made here in Frankfort. We are going to Canondale—or what was Canondale—at once."

By the time he arrived at the edge of the desolate wasteland, the police had had time to determine the extent of the blight. To their dismay, they had found that not only Canondale but three other small villages had ceased to exist, their every vestige lost in the almost colorless dust that spread over the sites on which they had stood. The spot that had been Canondale was near the outside of a circle of destruction—a circle in which no living thing seemed to survive; in which not so much as a post raised itself above the level of the ground. The center of that barren waste seemed to be at a point where a little hamlet called Stocktonville was located.

"I have been in that place, Operator 5," Jeff Darrow volunteered when Jimmy asked for information about the village. "A car that belonged to the Stocktons broke down in Canondale about six months ago. I repaired it, and Ruth and I drove out to deliver it. Stocktonville is way off by itself, a little place that's cut off from all the rest of the world. One time there used to be a mill of some sort there, but it was closed up years ago. The Stockton family owned the mill, and they just about own the village now. They live in a big house that looks like these pictures you see of old European castles, and everybody in the village works for them some way or another—on their farms or on the estate."

"A miniature reincarnation of feudalism here in Ohio," Ruth added. "I understand that the Stocktons wanted to keep it that way—wanted to prevent the modern world from encroaching on their little barony."

A village cut off from all the rest of the world and dominated by a family or a man with Old World ideas of living.... A village where any sort of deviltry might be hatched without word of it reaching the outside world.... Where a madman with anachronistic ideas of medieval pomp and power might hatch a wild scheme to set himself up as a king or emperor in democratic America....

Those disturbing possibilities flashed through Jimmy's mind, and he decided to investigate Stocktonville in the morning, as soon as it was light enough to start. That thought would give him no rest. All evening he debated it, and when black night had settled over the dusty desolation he strode out to the edge of the bleak waste.

Somewhere out in that inexplicable stretch of newly-made barrens, he felt certain, lay the answer to this mystery that mocked at America and all human understanding. Somewhere in that gray waste....

Suddenly his every nerve tingled, and his eyes strained out into the impenetrable darkness. As if in answer to his thoughts, a light, so faint that it was hardly discernible, had flashed out there in the wasteland. There it was again, barely visible but *certain* this time!

One faint flash after the other... the dot-and-dash beams of a magnesium flare. A blinker message that was being sent in a code known only to Diane Elliot, Tim Donovan and himself. So there *was* life out in that stricken desert! Diane or Tim was out there, striving to get word back to civilization and to reach him!

"Stocktonville... prisoner... Stocktonville," he picked out the words, while his pulses leaped. *"Held here by Henry G—"*

Jimmy strained his eyes until they ached and watered, but the flashes had stopped, the message abruptly cut off in the middle. That could have only one meaning.

The sender had been apprehended—captured or killed....

For long minutes that seemed like an eternity, he remained there, his burning eyes boring into the Stygian blackness. At last he was rewarded. The blinker was working again, and now there was no mistaking its message. It was from Diane—a call for help that gripped his heart with icy fingers.

"Prisoner here in Stocktonville... have been tortured terribly... condemned to die unless I lure you here," the phrases ate into his brain. *"Please stay away, Jimmy... if you love me!"*

Diane, sacrificing herself in order to warn him!

Jimmy whirled and raced for the farmhouse where the Darrows were being detained for the night.

WHEN HELL CAME TO AMERICA

CHAPTER 7
WHERE PATRIOTS DIE

HENRY GERBER'S car was powerfully motored, and he had driven with an utter disregard for speed limits. Yet it was hours before he reached his destination. Through parts of Virginia and West Virginia, Diane knew they had gone, and then she caught a glimpse of a town name she placed in Ohio. But Gerber was bound for no town. At long last the car rolled into a sleepy little village—a mere handful of cottages that were illuminated fantastically by the headlights.

Past these and into a tree-arched driveway that led to a big stone building the car glided, and now the aura of fantasy was even stronger. It was almost as if Diane had been wafted to one of those fairy lands of which she had dreamed when she was a child. This building was a veritable castle, a European château with towers and looming spires.

Beneath a wide archway and into an inner court Gerber drove. There he was greeted by four men who came running even before he had shut off his motor. Four men whose crisp military salutes respectfully greeted him.

"We have a guest tonight," he grinned. "In the back of the car. She does not feel up to walking, so perhaps you will carry her—to the 'reception room'."

Without betraying the slightest evidence of surprise, they opened the back door of the sedan and lifted her out. Diane was trundled into the building and to a bare stone cubicle—a mere cell with no furnishings but a cot that was covered only by a blanketed mattress. Gerber followed and dismissed them with a nod.

"I fear you will not find your quarters very comfortable tonight," was his elaborate pretense of solicitude. "You see, we were hardly prepared for you. Had we known that you were going to honor us, it would have been another matter. However—" he shrugged—"the night is almost over. Perhaps tomorrow we shall be able to make a more suitable arrangement for you. Yes—" he regarded her critically as he untied the rope that held her aching arms at her sides—"I do not doubt that we shall."

The sinister suggestion in his gleaming eyes was unmistakable, and Diane recoiled from the touch of his hands. But after freeing her arms he bowed mockingly and left her to untie her ankles and remove the gag. The heavy door thudded shut solemnly after him and a key grated in the lock, but Diane sighed with the mere relief of simply being out of his presence.

What sort of a place was this to which he had taken her? What did he intend to do with her? What awaited her in the morning? What were those 'interesting things' he had promised she would witness? And how could she escape or get word of her predicament to Jimmy?

DIANE HAD ample opportunity to debate that possibility, for the hours passed and nobody paid her any attention. Noon, one o'clock—and again the silent waiter appeared with her lunch. It was not until mid-afternoon that Henry Gerber, himself, put in an appearance.

"You must pardon me for my neglect." He favored her with

his mocking grin. "But we have been very busy all day. This is to be a red-letter day in American history. Yes, a *red* letter day!" he repeated significantly and chuckled at his witticism. "But now we are ready for you. Kurt Mahler is waiting to interview you."

Kurt Mahler, she discovered, was a beefy, red-faced man of about forty. A German, undoubtedly, she decided at once, and the moment he spoke his accent proclaimed his nationality unmistakably. He held court at a long table in what appeared to be a reproduction of a medieval dining-hall. Around him were grouped six other men, and still others came and went continually. These seemed to be Frenchmen—or were they Alsatians, like the man Kreiter, who had been killed while attempting to kidnap Ralph Kennedy from the hospital?

Mahler, it was apparent at once, was master of the place. All the others deferred to him, and even Gerber fawned upon him.

"This is the lady about whom I was telling you, *Herr* Mahler," Gerber smiled unctuously. "*Fraulein* Diane Elliot—whom, it is said, has more influence with Operator 5 than anyone in America."

Boldly the beefy Mahler's little, pig-eyes ran over her figure, inventoried her from head to foot—and Diane felt her cheeks flame. An angry outburst hovered on the tip of her tongue, but Mahler nodded with satisfaction and motioned her to a chair.

"The Operator 5—he has very good taste," he paid her his heavy, smirking compliment. "But he does not have much brains, this man." He shook his heavy head and drew a long face. "He should know better than to take chances with such a lovely *fraulein*. War is man's work, not for women—"

"War?" Diane picked him up quickly. "Who is at war with America? No nation," she answered her own question.

Her indignation carried her away, and she rose from her chair to stand in front of Mahler and fling her contempt in his face.

"You were eager enough to escape from Carliotti's tyranny—and this is your gratitude!" she scorned him. "Go back where you came from, the lot of you. We have no place for your kind in America. You may make trouble—may commit barbarous outrages—for a while. But you will be cornered, and when you are you will wish that you were back under Carliotti—"

"Carliotti!" several of them snickered, and she could see them winking at one another, laughing sardonically.

Vaguely she sensed that they were laughing at her—that there was something about Carliotti, about her mention of his name, that she did not understand. Something that afforded them vast amusement. But now Mahler was speaking and the others hushed.

"Such a lovely *fraulein* worrying about world politics!" he deplored. "It is a pity. Politics, like war—that is no business for a *fraulein*. We have other uses for women—far better uses—" he grinned with insulting significance—"especially for such a lovely one as the *fraulein*."

He turned to Henry Gerber. "To question this one about Operator 5 would only be a waste of time. I know this kind of woman. Gerber—they are very interesting, very interesting indeed... but not for questioning. Not now anyway. Perhaps after all she has seen, it will be different. Take her upstairs and entertain her, my dear Gerber. See that she does not want for amusement... until I have time for her."

Willingly Gerber took her by the arm and led her from the room—through corridors and up narrow stairways until they reached a small room in one of the towers. It was more comfortably furnished than the cell in which she had spent the night—so comfortable that she shuddered. This luxury, she knew all too well, was not for her—but for Kurt Mahler!

Gerber seemed to read her thoughts. Standing in the doorway with his arms folded on his chest, he gloated over her. He watched her as a snake watches a bird, as she walked to one of the narrow windows and looked out over the quiet countryside that was so close—and yet so far from her at that moment. It seemed that she could almost call down to the little village at the edge of the château estate, and yet it might have been a thousand miles away for all her chance of reaching it....

As she stared out of the window, a peculiar noise suddenly interrupted her dismal thoughts. A buzzing that sounded like the hum of a great dynamo. It grew louder and seemed to fill the whole building—seemed to press in on her eardrums. Questioningly she turned to Gerber, and found him smiling with an evil anticipation that he made no attempt to conceal.

"The red-letter day I promised you—it is starting," he chuckled. "I promised you, also, that you should see some interesting things—and I always keep my word. Come with me, and I shall show you."

That was a command rather than an invitation. His fingers fastened on her arm, and he led her out of the tower room, back into the main part of the large, sprawling building, and up into another tower that rose in the center of the structure and dominated all the others. Now the buzzing was even louder, so strong that it actually hurt her ears—and on the open top of that tower Diane discovered its source....

HALF A dozen men were on the bat-demented roof of that tower. Three of them were busily engaged with a queer contraption that looked like a huge telescope—a contraption that was mounted on a swivel and that was now aimed horizontally at the surrounding countryside. Three others stood at the edge of the low, crenelated wall, studying the scene through field-glasses. It was this intricate mechanical contraption from which the buzzing was issuing—so loud that the crew who served it wore guards over their ears.

"You will need these to enjoy the performance properly," Gerber shouted, and he handed her a pair of field-glasses taken from a rack beside the strange-looking mechanical contrivance. "Over there to the right, where the others are looking."

Automatically Diane lifted the glasses to her eyes—and instantly she froze, hardly believing what she saw. Once, as a child, she had seen a panorama of the Galveston flood in an amusement park—had watched, fascinated, as the rain beat down and the little buildings crumbled and were swept away. That was what she was seeing now—except that there was no rain and no flood!

Her glasses were trained on a little village that seemed to be miles off, and as she watched, the houses disintegrated and *melted* away. Not only the houses—the trees, the automobiles in the street, everything in the place. Even the people!

Horrified, she watched a dozen or more men and women trying desperately to outrun the destruction. But it caught up with them, swept over them—and they were no more! Utter destruction that erased everything; that wiped out the village as if it had never been and left nothing but a flat, gray waste in its wake!

And still the incredible destroyer ran on. Over fields and meadows, across roads and through clumps of trees, leveling buildings and the stone walls that surrounded them, gobbling up animals and luckless humans who were doomed before they knew what was happening. Before her unbelieving eyes Diane saw the countryside systematically, horribly, turned into an arid wasteland.

"Marvelous, isn't it?" Gerber's voice shouted in her ear. "All the work of this clever piece of mechanism—a death-ray such as America has never seen. From this tower we can sweep the surrounding country for miles—and nothing in God's world can stand against us!"

Slowly the infernal ray-projector was swinging around, was dipping and rising, bathing mile after mile with utter destruction. Appalled by the incredible horror she was witnessing, Diane stood there like one transfixed, staring with bulging eyes....

If only there was something she could do. If only she could stop that monstrous slaughter—could thwart this devilish machine before it spread its ghastly trail any farther. But she was

utterly helpless. There was nothing she could do but stand here and watch a horror such as no mortal had ever before witnessed.

But there *was* something she could do! She could smash that devilish projector! She could fling herself upon it, tear it apart with her bare hands, put it out of commission in some way!

Her eyes must have betrayed her. Henry Gerber was watching her like a hawk, and suddenly his fingers fastened like a vise on her arm. Tightly he held her while he took the field-glasses out of her hand and turned her back to the entrance in the floor of the tower.

"I think you have seen enough for a while," he taunted. "We'll give you a chance to think this over."

Back to the room in the corner tower he led her and left her there. Diane heard the door being locked behind him, but it meant nothing to her. Her eyes were still seeing that unbelievable, impossible destruction—her mind reeling under the necessity of believing what she knew could not be true but *was*, past all human doubting....

LONG HOURS she sat there, questioned her own sanity. Dully she realized that the all-pervading buzzing noise had stopped: realized that the sun had gone down, that it was night. Without interest she looked up as a guard appeared and brought a tray with her supper. Listlessly she turned away even before he had left the room. At the window she stared out at the deepening darkness.

Darkness—that was the answer! Suddenly she galvanized with inspiration. She could not possibly escape from that tower, but she might possibly get a message out of it! If she could open one of those narrow slits of windows, reach through it to the outside of the rock sill... that would be all she needed!

Quickly she lifted her skirt and unstrapped a small, high-powered magnesium flare which was fastened to one of her legs. She started to the window, then held herself sternly in check. It was still too light outside. She must be patient, must wait until it was entirely dark so that the magnesium beam would reach the maximum of its effectiveness.

That wait was the worst ordeal she had ever endured.... A thousand questions tortured her mind, as she counted the minutes and watched the sky becoming blacker and blacker. Would Jimmy Christopher see her blinker message when she sent it? There was one chance in a million he would be anywhere in that neighborhood. But at least it *was* a chance. He might have come to view the destruction of which word must have reached him by now. Or if he did not see it, perhaps someone else would. Someone who would report it to the authorities and from whom Jimmy would eventually receive notification.

She could only hope and pray... and then, at last, it was time!

In a few moments she had the flare propped up on the narrow sill, had the metal cover ready to break the blinding beam into the dots and dashes of the Morse code.... The beam shot outward and penciled a shaft of red light up into the night.

"Stocktonville... prisoner... Stocktonville," she coded off the name she had heard her captors calling the little village in which she was. *"Held here by Henry G—"*

That was as far as she got. Before she could spell out his name, Henry Gerber came leaping through the doorway, to fling himself across the room and yank her away from the window. His face was diabolical, the face of a crazed savage who runs amok. But slowly a change came over it. The fury faded—and into its place came a crafty leer, a twisted grin that widened until his features were wreathed with evil delight.

"Don't let me stop you," he urged. "Go right ahead and call

Operator 5. Perhaps he will come here and join us. What could be finer?"

Defiantly Diane glared at him, and in the depths of his gleaming eyes she saw new deviltry hatching.

"So you will not call him?" he leered. "Very well—I shall call him myself. Give me a copy of the code you were using."

Again Diane did not deign to answer him. But as she watched him she suspected that that was just what he wanted her to do. Now the evil delight on his vulpine features was unmistakable. Quickly he strode to the door and stepped out into the corridor, to hail one of Mahler's men. For a few moments she heard the murmur of his voice, and then he came back, to sit on the arm of an easy-chair and grin at her while the tip of his tongue played over his lips.

Now what fiendish plan had he hatched?

Her question was answered in a few moments when the door opened again and two men came in. Each dragged with him a young woman who was half-nude. Young girls whose faces were convulsed with fright, whose shamed eyes avoided Diane's when she looked at them. American girls—and Diane knew at once what their lot had been... knew how they had been kept here in the mansion-house to serve as playthings for these foreign beasts.

"These young ladies have come here to persuade you to change your mind," Gerber fairly purred. "They want you to give me that code, but if you won't—"

His hands streaked out and seized their scanty garments, ripped at them and stripped them to the waist. While the men held the whimpering, pleading captives helpless, he took thick strands of their long hair and tied them together—more than a dozen tight knots, so that they stood back to back, their heads within an inch of each other.

"Now let them dance," he commanded, and their captors released the victims—released them to draw sharp knives with which they prodded them mercilessly from every side.

Screaming in agony, the girls fell to the floor and writhed there. Frantically they tried to wriggle away from those devilish knives that sank an inch deep into their soft flesh. But every contortion almost tore the scalp from their heads. In a few moments the floor was wet and slippery with their blood. Moaning, they lay there, hardly able to squirm away from those relentlessly prodding points. Pleadingly, their tortured eyes sought Diane's, when Gerber at last gave them a respite.

"They do not seem to do very well on the knives," he frowned. "Perhaps we had better try fire. Go and get some fagots, Anton."

"No... no... no!" both victims screamed in unison. "Oh, don't let them burn us! No—no! Not the fire! *Please!*"

Their frenzied pleas rang in Diane's ears. Grim-eyed she had watched their ordeal, while her teeth bit right through her lower lip. And now she would have to watch them being seared and tortured with flaming fagots. Now she was condemning them to unendurable agony by refusing Gerber's demand. But to yield, meant betraying Jimmy—meant leading him into a trap that would be sure death....

ANTON HAD hardly left when he was back, bringing two foot-long faggots that blazed merrily. Diane watched them with horrified eyes as they pressed against the soft flesh—heard the hiss of searing blood, smelled the odor of burning flesh… and then she gave up.

"Stop—for God's sake, stop!" she capitulated. "I'll give you the code—anything, as long as they don't have to suffer anymore!"

Despising herself for her weakness, she sat down and made a transcript of the code that Jimmy Christopher would know could come only from her or from Tim Donovan. Feeling like a despicable traitor, she handed it to Gerber and sat there helplessly while he stepped to the magnesium beacon and rekindled it—to send out into the black night the cunningly worded message that would be certain to lure Jimmy to his death if he received it.

He finished and turned to face her triumphantly. "Now we will make preparations to receive him. There is plenty of time for that. First he must be allowed to get well into the waste we created this afternoon. Then, when it is too late for him to turn back, the ray will go to work again. It will be another spectacle for you to watch. Now perhaps I had better let you get some sleep so that you will be up early to keep watch with us in the morning!"

With a harsh chuckle Henry Gerber bowed himself out of the door.

POLICE OFFICERS were patrolling the edge of that stretch of desolation to prevent those who might be too curious from straying into the devastated territory. However, their presence was not necessary. None who came hurrying to gape at that astonishing gray wilderness had any desire to venture into it. Nobody would have dared to invade it after black night came down and added to its weird menace.... None but the Darrows.

Jeff and Ruth Darrow would have dared anything that night. In their breasts blazed an unquenchable hatred for whoever or whatever had swooped down and robbed them of their father and all their relatives and friends within a few short moments. Avidly they thirsted for revenge, for a chance to settle their grim score with whoever was responsible for this hell-spawned obliteration of a peaceful community.

Jimmy Christopher knew this when he hurried to the farmhouse where they were staying.

"I want to go to Stocktonville tonight—now," he announced. "Do you think you can guide me, Darrow?"

"Think? I *know* I can!" Jeff Darrow exploded. "You think that's where we'll find these murdering devils, Operator 5? You think they're hiding out in Stocktonville?" eagerly.

"I don't know—but that's what I mean to find out," Jimmy told him simply. "I am ready to start now, if you are."

"We are both ready," Ruth Darrow answered quickly, and he saw that she had already put on her coat and hat.

He shook his head regretfully. "I know how you feel," he said softly, "but this will be no trip for a woman. There is no telling what we may find out there—or what we may be going up against. I couldn't take you into that. Wait out here for us, and there may be some other way that you can serve."

Ruth started to object—but when she looked into his level blue eyes she knew that there was no use arguing. Operator 5 was not one to be swayed when he had made up his mind and was convinced that he was right. That would settle it, as far as he was concerned....

At the edge of the desolation they left her and plodded out into the gray waste that looked strange and fantastic in the beams of their flashlights. There was no use trying to follow what had been the road. Jeff set his course by compass and by hills and gullies, the few features of that despoiled countryside that had not been obliterated.

Once the lights of the guards patrolling the edge faded in the distance it was as if they two were the only living things in a world of utter stillness—and soft dust that smudged beneath their shoes and rose up to choke them. Not a sound did they hear for nearly an hour, and then Jimmy grasped Jeff's arm and froze him into silence.

There had been a sound behind them—a dull thud. And then there came the blast of a sneeze. Two more, as they whirled and swung their lights backward and charged down on a figure that floundered in the dust.

"Please!" Ruth Darrow wailed, as they pounced upon her. "I *had* to come after you. I couldn't stay back there alone. I was making out all right until I stumbled into that hole. I couldn't see it in the dark, and I didn't dare come any closer to you."

She had already amply demonstrated that she would be no burden to them, Jimmy considered as she stood anxiously awaiting his verdict. To take her back to the guards would mean the loss of nearly two hours—and perhaps there might be some way that she could serve better than a man.

With a grin of admiration for her courage, he agreed to let

her stay with them, and together the three of them now plodded on into the desolation. For what seemed endless hours they trudged through Stygian darkness, until is seemed that the desolate wilderness must never end—seemed as if all the world had been blighted by this gray pall.

But at last Jeff spied what he was certain was a momentary glimmer of light in the distance.

"There it is!" he whispered. "That must be Stocktonville just ahead of us... if there still is such a place."

More carefully now, they crept forward, using their flashes as little as possible. Eyes forward, straining for a repetition of that momentary speck of light, they staggered back as if struck a physical blow—when suddenly the desolate plain on all sides of them was brightly illuminated by a powerful searchlight that seemed to reach out over it for miles!

A trap! Too late Jimmy realized that they had walked into it!

Starkly outlined there in that pitiless light, they were easy targets for marksmen who could pick them off from the darkness. There was only one hope for them—to reach the low buildings of the little village they could see just ahead.

"We've got to run for it—fast as you can make it!" he yelled, and grabbed Ruth's arm to help speed her to cover.

Panting and choking from the penetrating dust, they staggered into the village and ran through what seemed to be its main street. The place appeared to be completely deserted. But suddenly Jimmy was aware of a weird, all-penetrating buzzing that filled the air—and there, within twenty feet of them, the entire line of cottages on one side of the street began to disappear—*to melt away into nothingness!* Fascinated, his legs robbed of all motive power, he stood and stared at that incredible destruction—realized with inexorable certainty that the thing which had doomed Governor Calhoun, and desolated this whole countryside, had been turned loose on them!

In a moment it would engulf them, and that would be the end....

CHAPTER 8
BLOOD OF AMERICANS

THERE HAD been no sleep for Diane Elliot when Henry Gerber bowed himself out of her tower room and locked the door behind him. For hours she had alternated between pacing the room and sitting on the edge of the divan that was to be her bed, peering out into the darkness and searching every corner of that prison room.

What now?

The promptness with which Gerber had interrupted her signaling had convinced her that the room was equipped with peepholes through which she could be watched. Yet now she was unable to locate them. Nevertheless, she could fairly *feel* those eyes observing her every move. To thwart them, she put out the light and sat in the dark.

That darkness was the blackest she had ever known. Inside the room and out, the Stygian gloom was not broken by the faintest trace of light... until suddenly the whole outdoors sprang into almost daylight brightness!

Diane ran to the window and peered out. Great searchlights mounted on the towers were bathing the entire countryside in blinding radiance, and instantly she understood their purpose. Jimmy Christopher must be down there somewhere, trying to come to her aid—and this pitiless glare would mean his certain doom!

Once those searchlights had picked him out, the fearful death-ray would be turned upon him and he would be melted away into nothingness! He hadn't a chance, unless she could help him—unless, somehow, she could keep that lethal ray away from him. But how—*how?*

Now her brain was spinning at top speed. A prisoner here in a locked room, she simply *had* to get out—*had* to go to Jimmy's rescue before they had a chance to cut him down. How…?

And then she had the answer! Into her whirling brain flashed a reminder of the peepholes with which she was certain the room was equipped!

Stepping back to the light-switch, she pressed the button and then half-ran to the table that stood in the center of the room. Down into the neck of her dress her hand dived, to come out with several sheets of paper and a pencil. Nervously she gnawed the end of the pencil while her eyes darted to the window. Then finally she began to write, hurriedly, feverishly.

Apparently she was absorbed in the composition of her note. But her nerves were tense, ears straining for the slightest sound, eyes watching from their corners. *There* was the sound she expected! The door was opening almost noiselessly. A man was stepping inside. With a rush he came charging across the room, grabbing to snatch the paper from her hand. His fingers closed on it, crumpled it—and then, to his amazement, he was swept off his feet, was sailing through the air, to land on the back of his neck against one of the baseboards.

Diane had moved like a flash. The moment his arm stretched out in front of her, she had seized it in a jiu-jitsu grip Jimmy Christopher had learned from one of the greatest Japanese masters of the science. Over her shoulder the guard had sailed—and the dull snap of breaking bones as he hit the floor told her that all resistance was gone from him.

Stooping over the limp body, she ran her fingers through his pockets and appropriated his automatic. Then she was out of the room, racing down the corridor to the stairway and heading for the central part of the building and the death-ray tower that rose above it.

How she could put that deadly projector out of commission she did not know. One girl against half a dozen or more husky men, she would have slight chance of overcoming its crew and capturing it. What she needed was a bomb or a grenade—a charge of high explosive that would demolish the thing. But to secure that was out of the question. There was nothing....

And then her eyes encountered a medieval mace that hung on the wall of the hall above a steel breastplate and helmet. That ancient war-club would have to serve her purpose! Tearing it from the wall, she ran on, uninterrupted, to the tower stairway, gaining the roof before shouting men came racing after her.

The ray-projector was in operation when she arrived, but the steel-spiked knob of the mace made short work of dispersing the crew. Howling and clutching their bleeding heads, they staggered back and gaped wide-eyed as she hammered and battered the delicate mechanical contraption. Before the observers could whirl and spring back from the edge of the parapet her work was finished. The humming drone had stopped, and the projector was reduced to useless ruins....

Kurt Mahler was one of those who had been watching the ray's diabolical work through field-glasses. With a yell of rage he leaped across the roof and seized her, knocked the automatic spinning from her hand and fastened his thick fingers in her throat. Cruelly he bent her head backward, to snarl down into her empurpling face as his cruel fingers ground into her neck.

The blood was pounding in Diane's ears, agonizing pains stabbing through her lungs. Mahler's face swam in a blur above her, and she knew that she was losing her senses—was going to die.

But suddenly the German thought better of it. His fingers loosened their hold and allowed her to gasp for breath.

"It would be a mistake to kill you so," he snarled. "That would be too easy—far too easy. We must make for you a death far better than that—something that will give you a long time to pay for the damage you have done here!"

Striding to the parapet, he looked down into the village and then whirled on his men savagely.

"There are only three of them," he snarled. "Go and get them. Bring me their heads—that is all I want!"

BUT ONCE the elimination of that ray-projector had given him a new and unexpected lease on life, Jimmy Christopher lost no time in seeking a place of safety. At first it seemed that the hamlet was deserted, but now he saw frightened faces peering out of several houses—the faces of men that disappeared as they were lashed and beaten back by leather whips.

Those men were prisoners, held in those buildings under guard—and if they were prisoners, of whoever controlled this place, they should make willing allies. The question was how to liberate them. Quickly Jimmy wrestled with that problem… and found a solution.

"I'm going to ask you to act as bait, Ruth," he outlined quickly. "We'll take that third house first because we can creep up on it without being seen. I want you to go to the door and knock. Smile at whoever answers and try to get him to step out. Jeff and I will take care of him then."

Ruth's eyes flashed, and she smiled confidently. Fearlessly she stepped up to the door he had indicated, while Jimmy and her brother crept up beside the house. Her fingers rapped against the door and she stepped back, waiting with a scrap of paper in her hand—waiting until a foreign-looking man opened up and stood regarding her curiously.

"I'm a stranger here," she smiled at him. "I am looking for a Mr.—Mr.—" she bent over the paper—"perhaps you can make out his name and tell me where to find him."

The fellow's eyes looked her over appreciatively. A grin spread over his face, and he stepped out… to go down without a sound as Jeff Darrow caught him around the knees and Jimmy Christopher's fingers closed around his throat.

Back into the building they dragged him—to knock him

Jimmy led them, step by step, through that inferno of gunfire!

sprawling across the room when he tried to break loose and draw a gun. Instantly Jeff was after him, beating him into unconsciousness while Jimmy turned his flash around the room and encountered a ring of anxious, frightened faces.

"Is this the only guard?" he demanded.

"The only one in here," one of the cowering wretches answered, "but there are many more up at the big house."

"One man, to watch more than two dozen of you," Jimmy counted that ring of faces. "And you let him get away with it?"

"There is no use trying to fight them," another whimpered. "There is no escape from here. Some have tried—and we saw them die. We saw them disappear right out of the street, and that was the end of them. There is no chance to fight them. Now we will all be beaten terribly for what you have done."

He was fairly weeping, but Jimmy Christopher strode over to him and upbraided him contemptuously.

"And you call yourself an American!" he lashed out. "A man who is willing to be a slave—to take orders and cringe before foreign masters! There are only three of us—two men and a girl—but we are going to clean out this nest of murderers. You are free now, and that weapon you are so afraid of is destroyed," he gambled desperately. "I am Operator 5, and I need volunteers. I don't want cowards or slaves. I want men!"

Out of the circle stepped a square-jawed young fellow with a thin face and dark, smoldering eyes—one whose cheek and forehead showed the scars of the guard's whip.

"I'm with you, Operator 5," he volunteered, "and so is the rest of this outfit, whether they know it or not. They'll be behind you—"

"There are men coming from the Stockton house!" Ruth called a warning from the window where she was keeping watch on the street.

Those men would be well armed. Once they reached the village they would command the street, making egress from the houses impossible. The only hope was to stop them before they left the Stockton grounds. In the few minutes that he had been in the hamlet, Jimmy had made a quick survey of the place, had spotted the vantage point from which the road to the street could be dominated. That was where he must go.

"All right, you take charge here," he snapped to the young volunteer and thrust the gun, that had been taken from the guard, into the fellow's hand. "I am counting on you to free the rest of your men in these other houses and then come to my support. Ruth—" he turned to the watching girl—"you stay here and help organize the men. Jeff and I are going to put a stop to that advance."

Two against there was no telling how many—the odds were overwhelming. But Jimmy had to take them—had to make a stand until the enslaved villagers could be freed and rallied. Even then, unarmed and broken in spirit as they were, he admitted that they would be of doubtful value....

The Stockton estate was separated from the village by a dry gully which had somewhat the appearance of a moat. Perhaps at one time there had been a stream in that gully. Now it was thoroughly dried up and filled with a rank growth of weeds and bushes. Perhaps, also, at one time a bridge had spanned it, but now part of the hollow had been filled in to make a dam-like road which connected the tree-lined driveway of the Stockton estate with the main street of the village.

It was this bottle-neck that Jimmy rushed to defend.

He and Jeff Darrow arrived barely in time. Already more than a score of men were swarming over the road. Flinging themselves down behind big trees on both sides of the village end, the defenders picked off their marks with deadly precision. Volleys of lead poured at them and pocked the trunks of the trees, but the marksmen were well concealed.

Jimmy counted nine of the on-coming detachment who dropped to the road or jumped, screaming, into the gully before their fellows broke and stampeded back to the protection of the estate. But then one of their leaders must have rallied them, and driven them back to the fray. On they came again—but this time Jimmy quickly detected that their rush was half-hearted, only a feint to hold the defenders' attention. The real attack was materializing on the flanks, up from the gully.

Grimly he watched the tell-tale rustle in the bushes. They were creeping up on him from one side, closing in on Jeff Darrow from the other.

"Watch yourself, Jeff—down in the gully!" he shouted a warning, and then leaned far over to trigger two shots at the flankers who were now dangerously close to him.

But to do this he had to expose himself dangerously. Lead blasted at him from the road, flung dirt up into his face, ripped through the sleeve of his coat. Back behind the shelter of the tree, he realized that he could not hope to defend his flank. The trap was closing on him. In a few moments they would rush, and he would have no choice but to spring to his feet and trade bullets with them until they cut him down....

"I see them—but I can't do anything about it," Darrow cursed soulfully, and Jimmy knew that his plight was equally critical.

Only a matter of minutes now... of seconds!

Three faces emerged from the bushes not more than twenty-five feet from him. Orange flashes pitted the night; lead whistled by his head. Jimmy tensed, ready to leap up and take as many of them as possible into the yawning jaws of death with him. Now....

But at that moment there was a wild yell behind him. Wonderingly, he wheeled—and beheld a motley rabble charging from the village. A mob of ragged men who were armed with knives, scythes, clubs, anything on which they could lay their hands. At their head ran Ruth Darrow and the young fellow to whom he had given the guard's gun. The released prisoners had found sufficient courage to charge against their oppressors!

A wave of pride surged through Operator 5 at that moment—pride that he was an American! A few minutes ago these men had been broken and cringing, quailing in the face of danger. Now they were coming on, almost unarmed, against they knew not what terrible weapons! Helpless slaves one moment, heroes the next—and the secret was the unconquerable American blood that pumped through their veins!

RUTH DARROW had had much to do with that transformation. Her scornful words had cut the fear-ridden men to the quick, stabbing through the terror that gripped them. Her example had shamed them into following her, grimly determined to die rather than be reduced once more to abject slavery.

Straight toward the road to the estate they charged. But

even before they reached it, Ruth saw what was happening and understood the momentous decision she must make, the agonizing choice that confronted her. The men from the estate were closing in from both sides, overwhelming Jeff and Operator 5. Flinging her ragged legion into the fray, she might be able to save one of them—but not both!

Operator 5 was already on his feet, crouching behind the tree, poised and ready to meet to his death. Jeff was on his knees, hugging the trunk of his shelter as he leaned forward to empty his weapon into the oncoming faces. In that moment of crucial decision, his figure seemed to swim before Ruth's eyes. Suddenly she saw him again as a boy—as they used to play together; as he was that day he had saved her from drowning, as he was the time he had stood up to a bully twice his size and taken a brutal beating to shield her. Jeff, her brother, her last living relative.... But behind that other tree was Operator 5, the man who more than once had snatched America from the brink of ruin. The man the country needed now more than ever before, who alone was equipped to battle this incomprehensible menace that loomed over the nation....

In that bitter moment Ruth Darrow faced her Gethsemane. Cruelly torn between sisterly love and duty, she hesitated—and her brother took the decision out of her hands. He, too, had realized the choice she must make... and now he made it for her.

Leaping from behind his tree, he sprinted across the road calling loudly.

"Follow me!" he shouted to the oncoming rescuers—and then he was in front of Operator 5, hurling himself at the enemy.

Straight down into the gully he charged. Snarling faces rose out of the bushes all around him. Pistols blazed at him. Lead stabbed through him like searing irons, staggered him. But he kept on his feet. Like a bloody flail his empty automatic rose and fell, smashed into faces and over skulls—until he could hardly lift his arm... and all the world became a wild kaleidoscope veiled by a red, dizzy haze.

Behind he dimly heard the wild shouting, the crashing of men charging into the bushes. The noise was becoming fainter, fainter... and even before his bullet-ridden body slumped and rolled into the gully Jeff Darrow was dead.

They trampled him underfoot, but his gallant sacrifice had not been in vain. In that split-second he had not only saved Operator 5 for America, but he had turned the tide of that desperate struggle. His inspiring example served to restore the manhood of even the most broken-spirited of the erstwhile prisoners. Rallying to Jimmy Christopher, they swept down into the gully and drove the foreign oppressors in utter rout before them. Then they turned to meet the detachment from the other side of the road.

That clash was short, sanguinary. Knives and scythes and pitchforks against rapid-firing automatics—the advantage was all with the foreigners. But Kurt Mahler's men had no stomach for the cold steel that licked out at them, no heart, either, to face the reckless charge of those desperate madmen. They broke and fled back to the estate—did not stop running until they had gained the sanctuary of the stone building and the heavy doors had closed behind them.

Around the building the villagers swarmed. Now there were nearly two hundred of them—raging avengers ready to take this inhuman fortress to pieces with their bare hands.

"They have our women in there," Frank Gillette, the grim-faced youth whom Jimmy had made his lieutenant explained. "I was only married a week when they came. They tore Mollie out of my arms and left me lying in a ditch. When I came to my senses I was herded into a slave gang with the rest of the men—and our women were all in there, to wait on those devils and become their playthings. Now that the men are free, we'll have a hard time holding them in check. They want to storm the doors."

Jimmy debated that problem, soberly. He had close to two hundred men, but only half a dozen had firearms—the automatics taken from their guards. He did not know how many there might be in the Stockton house, but he was certain that they were well armed—perhaps with weapons he did not even suspect.

Should he wait until he could send a messenger through the barren wasteland to summon help? Should he hold back until artillery could be brought in to blast the imitation castle to pieces?

Before then that deadly destruction, which had stopped so inexplicably, might recommence. It would mean curtains for all of them—a horrible end for Diane at the hands of her bestial captors. He must strike now, at once—capture the building and put an end to the menace before these devils had a chance to reorganize.

Maneuvering carefully into position, he took aim at one of

those blinding searchlights and shattered it. One after the other, he put them out of commission—all except the one mounted on the central tower. And this was unable to direct its beam onto the grounds close to the building.

Under the cover of darkness the villagers went to work. Dragging up ladders and wagons, they built approaches that reached almost to the top of the towers. But it was dawn before they were ready to attack.

JIMMY CHRISTOPHER led the way. Mounting the makeshift scaffolding, he waited until his men were in position around two of the towers—then gave the word. Like human flies they swarmed over the building, working their way from crevice to crevice in the rough stone. Noiselessly they climbed, and Jimmy began to hope that they might take the place by surprise—when suddenly a hoarse bellow boomed out above him.

"You down there!" Kurt Mahler shouted. "So you come for your women, do you? All right—then we give them to you. Here they are!"

A terrified scream slashed through the early morning stillness and was echoed by a chorus of frightened cries—by the mocking laughter of heavy voices. Now the tower tops were swarming with men. Jimmy saw their devilish intention. On the edge of the parapet was the young woman from whose throat those terrified screams pealed. Her arms were tied behind her, her horrified eyes staring down aghast at the sheer drop. Two men had hold of her, and another was busy at her back.

"Now!" he gave the order—and she was flung over the edge!

Jimmy caught one glimpse of her terror-contorted face as she flashed past him—caught a glimpse of what seemed to be a round metal cylinder that was fastened between her shoulder-blades... *and then she was blown to pieces before his eyes!*

That metal cylinder was a bomb! A bomb that had taken a deadly toll among the attacking villagers! Now other women were being dragged to the edge of the towers. Their screams filled the air—ending in piercing shrieks as they hurtled out into space.

Human bombs raining death upon their loved ones!

Suddenly icy fingers closed around Jimmy's heart and seemed to drain it of blood. Rigid, he stared up at where Diane hovered on the stony brink. Two of the fiends had hold of her. Now a beefy-faced devil, apparently their leader, leaned over the edge.

"This one is for Operator 5!" he shouted—and pointed a gun point-blank at the head of the man now climbing frantically toward him. Jimmy saw that muzzle trained upon him. Desperately he lunged his body to one side and almost lost his precarious hold. Clinging to the rock with slipping fingers, he spidered upward as the shot roared almost in his ear—and in the same moment he reached the top!

Two men sprang to meet him, but he plunged past them as he vaulted over the parapet. Straight toward Diane he dived, to snatch the sputtering fuse from the bomb at her back. With bone-crushing force his automatic came down on the head of one man who held her; the other he shot squarely through the center of the forehead.

Their bodies were toppling over the edge when he whirled

and threw himself at the big man who came lunging at him. Face to face they met, stood there trading blows. The big fellow's beefy face twisted with venomous rage; his pig eyes glittered murderously. Curses snarled from his thick lips, and he lashed at Jimmy's head savagely with a heavy Luger pistol.

But Jimmy was ready. His eyes gleaming with a deep and abiding hatred for this beast and all he represented, Jimmy drove him back, tricked him into a sudden lunge—then brought down the automatic in a quick, chopping blow that split the other's skull.

For a tense moment Kurt Mahler's men had made no attempt to come to his aid. Fascinated by that death struggle, they had stood watching… until their leader fell. Then they closed in on the victor with a concerted rush, rabid wolves lusting to tear him to pieces.

HALF A dozen Americans had followed Jimmy over the parapet, and others were breasting the edge, bravely following his lead—but they were insufficient to meet that rush. Two of them went down. Others, trying to step over the wall, were hurled backward and sent pitching headlong to their death. Desperately Jimmy tried to hold his ground, to protect Diane with his body as he was pressed steadily backward. In a few moments, he knew, he would be overwhelmed. He and the few survivors would be forced to the edge, thrust over by sheer weight of numbers….

With berserk fury he flung himself forward in a last desperate charge. Then he was amazed to see the tower's defenders suddenly turn frightened faces from him; and swing toward the rear, where shots and the clash of steel were now echoing!

Out of the tower doorway swarmed a tattered aggregation of grim-faced fighters who followed close in the wake of Ruth Darrow. Butcher-knives vied with axes and sharp-bladed sickles, in the slaughter that followed. Red-tined pitchforks dove to reach their victims before skull-smashing clubs could be hammered home on luckless heads. Pistols meant nothing in that primitive struggle—the enraged Americans brushed them aside and closed in with the weapons their pioneer forefathers had used in generations past.

It was a fearful toll those weapons took!

The tower defenders went down on every side, until the roof was slippery with blood. Fleeing in wild panic from those merciless avengers, some were pressed back against the parapet—even leaped off into space in their frenzy to escape!

Those ruthless killers had given no mercy, and now they received none. They died, to the last man, on that tower roof. And as they died Ruth Darrow smiled a tight-lipped smile; a bitter, mirthless smile that fed on the memory of gentle old Doctor Eli's lifeless body slumped in her arms....

Back through the tower door and the rest of the building Jimmy Christopher led his victorious host. But their work was already well done. Creeping through a disused underground drain that Ruth Darrow had discovered with the aid of an old villager, they had fallen upon the defenders from the rear and taken them completely by surprise. In a few minutes death had wiped the lower floors clean, and now the only resistance came from the second of the towers the Americans were besieging. Yet even that resistance was already doomed.

When Jimmy led his men forward, to take the tower from below, he found the lower floors a blazing inferno through which no man could hope to pass. Hungrily the flames were leaping and spreading through the tindery inside of the old building; and in a few minutes it would be ablaze from top to bottom.

With consternation Diane eyed the spreading flames.

"This place holds the answers to many of our questions," she lamented, "but there is one thing we must try to salvage, Jimmy. On the roof of the central tower they have the ray-projector that reduced this whole countryside to a barren waste—"

"A ray-projector!" Jimmy Christopher exclaimed. "We've *got* to save that no matter if death itself—"

He did not have to call for volunteers; they swarmed around him. Eagerly they trooped after him to the ray tower. While some sought to hold back the encroaching flames, others tugged and tore at the disabled projector. Finally they succeeded in prying it loose and carried it down to safety. But Diane did not wait to see that accomplished.

The Stockton building and its secrets were doomed, but there still remained another way in which the riddle of this unprovoked attack on an unsuspecting country might be read. Kurt Mahler! She had seen him go down when Jimmy's automatic struck his skull, but he might not be dead.

Perhaps he still breathed, still could answer their questions.

With half a dozen men she climbed back to the corpse-littered roof of the tower and found the beefy-faced commander where he had propped himself up against a wall. He was not dead, but one look at his ashen, blood-smeared face revealed that he had not long to live. His eyes were already blurred, yet still they kindled with animosity when they recognized her.

She was silent.

Between them, the men lifted him and maneuvered his heavy bulk down the narrow tower stairs. Barely escaping the trapping flames, they reached the bottom and carried him out of the burning building.

But Kurt Mahler showed scant appreciation for having been snatched out of a blazing furnace. Vindictive hatred gleamed in his little eyes as he glared up at Jimmy Christopher. His blood-streaked, putty-white face twisted into a hideous mask—and with his dying breath he gasped a threat that sent a chill through all who heard him.

"You Americans!" he sneered. "What chance have you? This 'victory' today—it will only bring the end for you quicker. In a month all your fine country will be like that waste out there—from ocean to ocean...."

He died.

CHAPTER 9
THE SWORD FALLS

JIMMY CHRISTOPHER tried hard to persuade himself that that had been merely the spiteful threat of a dying man. But Mahler's words hung over his head like a Damoclean sword and would give him no peace. Instinctively, he realized that the man had been making no idle boast. Mahler had had something definite in mind—and it must be rooted out before his prediction materialized.

The few prisoners who had escaped the fate of their comrades in the Stocktonville stronghold proved to be surly, tight-lipped. Jimmy questioned them patiently, but stubborn silence rewarded his every attempt to break through their reticence. Even the threat of swift death before a firing-squad made no impression upon them, and finally he gave up.

Under heavy guard they were marched through the arid waste and then taken east, to New York. There they were investigated and identified. As Diane had suspected, every one of them, including the dead Mahler, proved to be a refugee from France who had fled to the United States in order to escape the tyranny of Evan Carliotti. All had been helped to the shores of America by Julius Schirmer's refugee aid committee.

That startling discovery dumbfounded the old philanthropist.

"It seems impossible," he shook his head perplexedly as he put on his reading glasses and peered at the record Jimmy presented to him. "Conditions in Europe are so terrible, it would seem that these people we have helped to escape should become model citizens—once they have the opportunity to enjoy the freedom of America. Why they should plot to make trouble here—"

He smiled wryly. "But perhaps my years have not given me a very deep understanding of human nature, Operator 5. I placed implicit trust in Henry Gerber. He was my secretary for nearly ten years. In many ways he was like a son to me—and now you tell me that he was a kidnaper and murderer, a traitor who consorted with foreign plotters and trouble-makers. It still seems hard to believe that he could have had anything to do with that infamous outrage in Times Square."

It was not until Kurt Mahler was dead that Diane had thought of Henry Gerber—and by then the Stockton mansion had been a huge bonfire with flames licking from every window and lapping around the towers. Jimmy had made a quick check-up, but Gerber was not among the prisoners—and it was too late to search the blazing building for his body.

The news of his death had effected Julius Schirmer profoundly, and now Jimmy referred to him guardedly.

"Did Gerber have anything to do with the selection of the immigrants who were to be helped by your committee?" he asked gently.

"Yes." The gray-haired, patrician head nodded sorrowfully. "He handled all the detail work—made the final selection from those recommended by our agents abroad. But—" he added hopefully—"these people are all very carefully investigated by our European inspectors."

"And who has charge of those inspectors?" Jimmy followed up quickly. "Who appointed them?"

"Henry Gerber," came Schirmer's reluctant admission.

But, after he had left the philanthropist's Park Avenue home, Jimmy still puzzled over that perplexing problem. Even though Gerber's guilt was established beyond question, he still could not understand why these Frenchmen and Alsatians, fleeing from the wrath of Carliotti, should come to America and immediately start conspiring against the country that had given them refuge.... Unless once more the wily Carliotti had scored by shipping his *agents*—not those he had oppressed—to the United States to work the mischief he had been unable to accomplish by more direct means.

Carliotti's agents using Schirmer's committee as a blind to be smuggled into the country as refugees, then banding together and plotting to overthrow the government.... With help from the murderous dictator they might be conducting this reign of terror, this assault by invisible bombers and deadly ray-projectors—to beat America to its knees and force the nation to accept the yoke of Carliotti once before rejected!

Back in Washington, Jimmy Christopher had little time to pursue these conjectures. Wholeheartedly he threw himself into the research work in Norman King's laboratory. Day and night they labored over the ray-projector—and at last they discovered its secret.

"An atomizer—that's the answer," King announced, when the projector was repaired and had been tested on a desolate spot on the shore of Chesapeake Bay. "An atomizer so powerful that it destroys the last vestige of molecular cohesion. Everything that comes within its sweep is utterly destroyed because it disintegrates to the minutest particles—is reduced to nothing but dust and gases."

Walking over to where a wooden building, a great rock and an old cannon had been standing before the ray was turned upon them, he stooped and ran his fingers through the silt-like dust that was all that remained. For long moments he stared at that

HENRY GERBER
KURT MAHLER
JULIUS SCHIRMER
WOLF TAUGMAN

NAN CHRISTOHER
RALPH KENNEDY
RUTH DARROW
JEFF DARROW

fine gray residue—and when he turned back to Jimmy his grave eyes harbored a fear he made no effort to conceal.

"This is a fearful invention, Jimmy," he said in a voice that was hushed with awe. "Developed a bit farther, this machine can make an arid desert of the entire world and destroy every vestige of life!"

Every vestige of life except that which was hidden and protected by the shroud of near-invisibility a sample of which Jimmy had salvaged from the bomber that had been brought down in Washington. Norman King and his associates had spent long hours over that precious sample, and gradually they had identified the elements that went into the mystifying preparation.

At first their attempts to reproduce it were feeble and ineffective, but finally they had discovered the formula and evolved a dye which rendered garments almost entirely invisible at a distance of more than twenty-five or thirty feet.

"It is a partial reversal of the polaroid principle," King had explained. "Where two sheets of polaroid crossed at right angles will blot out all light and become opaque, the elements we use here, working against each other, blot out all color and produce an illusion of invisibility. We can incorporate this protective dye in a cream to be applied to the skin, can fuse it into glass for goggles. It can be used as paint to cover wood or metal—for that matter, practically anything can be rendered nearly invisible by it."

Now King had brought along a suit of the "invisible" clothes which he draped on a scarecrow and set up as a target for the ray-projector. Standing in the middle of the gray dust patch, the scarecrow faced the withering blast. The projector began to hum, increased in volume until its drone filled the air before King snapped it off.

But when Jimmy ran out to investigate the wood-and-clothes martyr, the scarecrow still stood intact, except that the top of the upright and the ends of the crosspiece had disappeared where the wood extended beyond the invisibility-treated cloth.

That dye-treated cloth was impervious to the ray's deadly beam!

"So that is why the dust clouds that chased the Darrows were able to walk through the desolation that had been Canondale," Jimmy Christopher understood at last. "They could stroll unharmed right through the ray that was blasting everything around them."

He was elated with his discovery, but Norman King's sober face was a picture of despair. "Now I begin to comprehend the full significance of the coupling of these terrible weapons," he thought aloud. "All the world and every vestige of human life can be wiped out with this machine—all except that which is protected by a veneer of invisibility. It promises a wonderful future for our descendants, Jimmy. Our generation will bequeath to them a drab, misty-gray world—in which swift death will be the portion of anyone who dares to appear in the bright, normal colors with which the Creator painted this earth!"

DR. KING and his associate scientists could produce this dye in limited quantities, but they did not have the equipment necessary for wholesale production. To erect the factories and install the required equipment would take weeks, months—and now every second was infinitely precious.

Jimmy Christopher debated that problem and finally turned to the nation's industrial leaders for the answer. In Julius Schirmer his appeal met a prompt response. The old man, although retired from any of the enterprises which had built up his fortune, was still chairman of the board of directors and absolute master of the largest chemical works in America.

"The services of the plant and staff of Consolidated Chemical are yours, Operator 5—I place them at your disposal," he volunteered at once. "Our scientists are among the best in the world, our staff of workers all expert in their line. We can produce this dye for you in almost any quantity you require—and we can treat the cloth right there in our plant. In fact—" he considered thoughtfully—"I know of an empty factory very close to our buildings in Newcastle. We can take that over and manufacture the uniforms there, without the loss of time that will be necessary if the cloth has to be shipped back to another city." He nodded.

"No, don't thank me," He held up his hand in protest when Jimmy attempted to voice his appreciation. "What I am offering is nothing more than should be expected of any American. It is the least I can do," he sighed wearily, "to help undo the mischief of my former secretary."

Schirmer's offer left Norman King and his men free to work on the problem of the disintegration ray.

"I want you to give me a super-ray, Doc," Jimmy told him. "One twice, three times, as strong as this one. I want one so strong that I can use it to wipe the others off the face of the earth and destroy this appalling menace for all time."

The third night after the fall of the Stocktonville stronghold he saw even more clearly that the fate of America would depend on King's ability to obey.

That night the airplane detectors around New York gave warning of powerful motors in the air—vibrations far stronger than any ever picked up before. The shrill alarm sirens screamed their warning, and thousands of terrified citizens rushed to the doubtful protection of supposedly bomb-proof underground shelters. Once more the vigilant Suicide Squadron members took to the air, guided to their invisible objectives by the keen mechanical ears in their rear cockpits—but this time they were destroyed before they could make their suicide dives and wreck the enemy.

Some of them exploded in mid-air; others simply vanished into space as if the heavens had opened to swallow them. In a few short minutes the tragedy-filled sky was empty—but no shower of death plummeted down upon the helpless city below. The destroying invaders winged on without a hostile gesture.

From Philadelphia the same reports came to Washington... from Pittsburgh, Columbus. And then Jimmy picked up the telephone and listened to a frantic call from Cincinnati.

"We're doomed, Operator 5!" his agent, Ben Gordon, fairly shouted over the wire. "They were overhead ten minutes ago! They wiped out all our planes! That seemed to be all—*but now the city is going down!* Cincinnati is being destroy—"

Abruptly that panic-ridden voice stopped. There was a dull

thud, and the line was dead. For nearly an hour Jimmy tried in vain to reestablish the connection, to reach other Cincinnati numbers—but the city seemed to be cut off from the rest of the world.

"There is no answer," the harried operator told him again and again. "I can't understand it. Cincinnati doesn't respond at all. I don't even get a buzz over the line."

But Jimmy Christopher could understand it, all too well....

Stunned by what he knew was the awful truth, he still would not admit that it could be possible until he flew over Cincinnati in an Army plane the next morning... and saw that the city no longer *existed!* Cincinnati had been wiped out as completely as little Canondale—and now a gray desert smudge blotted the rich center of the American Mid-West like a leper spot! And like a leper spot, Jimmy knew that it would spread....

"Until it reaches from ocean to ocean!" Kurt Mahler had promised.

CHAPTER 10
THE DEATH OF A NATION

THAT GREAT waste spot widened appallingly, and with its widening mad panic seized America. Towns and villages were gobbled up; square miles of fertile, fruitful land were turned into a barren desert waste. Waves of terror-ridden people fled frantically from the path of the on-coming destruction. Leaving everything behind in their feverish rush to escape, they sped in every direction. Like wildfire, the terror spread with them.

Men who were unafraid of death because arrant cowards in the face of this dread doom that would consume them and leave not even the shell of their bodies to be buried. They quailed from this fate against which nothing could protect them—sought frenziedly for an escape, for an assurance of safety that nobody could give them.

Operator 5 saw their panic, and his heart went out to them. But there was nothing he could do—nothing except attempt once more to speed the preparations he was making. It had taken time to remodel and equip Schirmer's factories for their new task, but the work had been accomplished with remarkable speed. Now they were producing the life-saving compound, and were increasing their output daily.

Once more Jimmy and Norman King hurried to the Chesapeake shore when the first specimens of that dye arrived. They held their breath while the projector played its deadly beam on the dyed suit of clothing they rigged in front of it... but the garments still remained unharmed!

"Thank God for that!" Jimmy gasped his relief. "We've done it, Doc! We've beaten the devils at their own game! With Schirmer's factories going at full speed, it will be only a few weeks before we can make every American soldier ray-proof! Only a few weeks more until we can extend the protection to every man, woman and child!"

But before there was time to fashion the newly dyed cloth into uniforms and to produce the invisibility tinctured ointment that would shield the human skin, another crushing disaster dealt the nation a staggering blow. Without waiting for orders from Washington, one General Sam Townsend had foolishly led three divisions of the Ohio National Guard up to within half a mile of the great waste stretch, and started to entrench there. Hardly had the troops encamped, scarcely had their picks begun to break the earth, than the scourge struck—swiftly and terribly.

In a few minutes the withering destruction had leaped over that intervening half mile and held the militiamen within its grasp. Over the half-built breastworks it swept, through the newly laid-out camp and the village beyond, where Townsend had his headquarters—and, wherever it reached, men ceased to be. Soldiers, military equipment, buildings… everything vanished, crumbled into dust.

The only survivors of those three divisions were the members of supply companies who were still coming up from the rear. They leaped from their trucks and fled wildly when they caught a glimpse of the doom that was enveloping their distant companions. Eye-witnesses of that fearful destruction, they were the first to spread the terrible news.

Nearly seventy thousand men evaporated into thin air! America reeled under that blow, and the flight from the threatened regions became a tremendous exodus that threatened to depopulate half of Ohio, Indiana and Kentucky. Like ripples on a lake the terror spread and the trembling populace sped before it.

"The poor, blind fool!" Jimmy Christopher groaned when that calamitous news reached him. "He slaughtered those men—dangled them like bait in the face of certain death!"

There was no hope of checking that all-consuming scourge at the edge of the wasteland—that was apparent. If a stand was to be made, it must be farther back, where there would be some chance to prepare a defense. Yielding hundreds of square miles to the implacable doom, Jimmy laid out a series of fortifications that would rival France's once-famed Maginot Line—a great semicircular line of concrete entrenchments and underground galleries from which an invisibility-protected army could hope to turn the tide against the unknown invaders.

By then, truckloads of the new uniforms were beginning to arrive. Supplies of paint for the concrete pillboxes were due shortly.

Supplies of ointment and goggles for the defenders were on the way. Day and night thousands of men toiled to complete the long, labyrinthian fortress.

That work was well in hand, capably supervised by the Army engineers. Jimmy's presence was no longer necessary—and yet there was a place where he was needed.... Out there in that powdery gray wasteland!

OUT THERE somewhere the hosts of the enemy were encamped. Where, he did not know, for every attempt to scout them from the air had failed. A score of Army planes had winged out over the desolation—and not one had come back. But where the planes had failed, half a dozen scouts on foot, protected by the new invisible equipment, might succeed.

Jimmy called for volunteers, and the response almost swamped the shack he was using for headquarters. He made no attempt to minimize the danger they would face, but scores still clamored to go with him.

"I'd like to take you all, but half a dozen men will be more effective out there than an army," he told the disappointed applicants. "What I want primarily are men who know the territory into which we will be going—men who *did* know it before it was transformed into a desert."

Six Ohioans who burned with a desire to come to grips with the despoilers who were laying waste their state, and Operator 5—clad in the new, dye-treated uniforms, their hands and faces salved over with the concealing ointment, they drove to the edge of the gray wilderness and stepped out into it. Anxiously Jimmy scrutinized them as the barrens closed around them, and what he saw satisfied him. Spread out fanwise, at a distance of twenty-five feet from one another, they were nothing more than indistinct blurs that were lost against the colorless background.

For hours they plodded into that desolate wilderness, striking for what Jimmy figured to be its center. The dust rose around them in little clouds, billowed into their faces when the wind gathered momentum over the unobstructed plain. Dim, ghostly shapes, hardly visible to one another, they might have strayed away and been lost in that fantastic gray world if Jimmy had not sounded a low whistle which brought them together at intervals.

The afternoon sun sank deeper and deeper. Dusk came on, and now total invisibility enveloped them. More frequently Jimmy sounded his whistle and counted his little company. As night closed down those assemblages became more eerie—gatherings of specters, with voices answering him out of nowhere.

TIM DONOVAN

Again and again they converged, and then, just as he was about to blow his whistle, Jimmy's nerves tensed and his puckered lips froze.

His keen ears had caught a sound from somewhere out there ahead of them. The clink of metal plates—the tell-tale sound of an encampment! A large encampment, he knew, as they cautiously crept closer and the noises became louder and more unmistakable.

"Down in the dust," he gave the order. "Crawl as close to the ground as you can. Drop flat on your bellies when you are within sight of anything. We've got to separate now. Take care of yourselves."

With a whispered farewell they were gone. Forward again, slowly and tediously now, he worked his way, but soon he could descry something ahead of him—the murky outline of large, tent-like shapes silhouetted against the darkening sky. Still forward, and then, to his immense gratification, he discovered that the ground near the encampment had not been utterly denuded like the surrounding territory. There was still some grass and low clumps of shrubbery.

Taking advantage of these, he crept close enough so that he could make out the indistinct outlines of a number of tremendous-sized planes. Around them he picked out the moving shadows that were men—crawled still closer until he could see them quite distinctly.

They wore colorless gray uniforms and peculiar goggles that caught his attention immediately—goggles with lenses that were balled outward like half-oranges. Those goggles.... He studied them intently, watched the surety with which the men walked about the camp, passing close to one another without even a near-collision. Even in that half-night they could see one another clearly—and in that moment he guessed their secret.

Those goggles were a part of their equipment he had to have!

Patiently he waited for his opportunity; waited until one of the men should be separated from the others. And then he saw his chance! One of them was stepping outside the camp to empty his plate.

Crouching low, Jimmy darted from behind the bush that sheltered him, reached another close to where the fellow must pass. Tensely he waited, his muscles taut—and then he leaped, bringing his automatic down on the man's head. He caught the falling body and dragged it behind the shrub.

Had he been seen? For long moments he crouched there, expecting to see shadowy figures come running toward him. Then he reached out and took the unconscious man's goggles, put them on in place of his own—and instantly the entire scene changed!

AS HE had suspected, those half-globular goggles were made of some material that overcame the invisibility of the dye that shrouded that camp to ordinary eyes. Now he could see the tents and the great transport ships plainly; could see the Teutonic-looking men who thronged the place. He could see them plainly... and suddenly he realized that *they* were able to see *him!*

Crouching even lower behind the fringe of shrubbery, he stripped off the fellow's uniform and donned it in place of his own. Now, dressed like the others, he would have some chance of passing among them unsuspected, would have an opportunity to investigate that amazing encampment.

One look at the broken skull of the man he had downed assured him that the fellow would be unconscious for several hours, if indeed he ever came back to his senses. Jimmy pushed the inert body farther under the branches and then stepped out boldly, swinging the empty tin plate at his side.

Nobody interfered with him as he advanced into the camp. None suspected the amazement with which he viewed it.

A complete military layout he found there. Lines of company streets in orderly rows, cook-tents and supply depots, headquarters pavilion—and an aviation section that fairly made his eyes pop. Nearly a score of huge, seven-motored transport planes stood side by side. These planes mounted no guns but were armed with deadly ray-projectors that nosed out of a specially constructed under-cabin in the belly of each ship.

Each of those ships could transport hundreds of men, which accounted for the small army around him. Fully two thousand, he estimated there were—two thousand Germans, by their guttural language and the Teutonic cast of their faces. In front of those huge ships were batteries of mobile ray-projectors, deadly weapons mounted on fast whippet tanks that could transport them with the speed of an average motor-car.

Amazement and consternation filled Jimmy Christopher as he eyed those massed destroyers. Such a terrible means of wholesale destruction had never been assembled in all the history of mankind... and here it was gathered to harry a nation that was at peace with the world. America had no quarrel with Germany, and yet the nationality of these invaders was unmistakable. They were German soldiers, even though the strange uniforms they wore were not those of the German army.

No matter why they were there, the immediate problem was to meet the appalling menace they represented—and Jimmy realized that the frantic preparations upon which the country was depending were woefully inadequate. It would take months to prepare to meet this onslaught, and America had only hours to steel herself for the test....

Near the line of gargantuan transports stood the big marquee which was the commander's headquarters. Protected with the invisible dye like the rest of the encampment, it was situated on a little hillock that overlooked the campsite on all sides. As Jimmy stared at it, a tall, square-shouldered figure stepped through the doorway and stood looking down at the activity below—a dour, brooding figure with a stern face that seemed to be all high forehead and sagging jowls... a fleshy face that was reminiscent of Germany's Iron Chancellor, Prince von Bismark.

"The wolf looks down on the fold," a man near Jimmy chuckled to his companions, but they quickly rebuked him.

"Wolf Taugman has ears everywhere," one of them warned, "and he does not appreciate jokes—unless you make them with bombs and death-rays! He is not looking down at you, little man. He sees far off in the distance where the Americans are running for their lives. Yes, I know what he sees—the hour when we swoop down on them and wipe them out by the thousands, the millions... that is what Wolf Taugman sees."

Wolf Taugman! A high-ranking officer in the German army,

he was the man to whom Fuehrer Franz Schnabel's racial extermination doctrines were attributed. Some years ago he had written a book on the theory of war which had shocked the world by its utter callousness—and he was the man who was commanding this murderous horde!

Standing there within a hundred yards of the marquee, Jimmy Christopher debated the possibility of making a desperate attempt to reach that monster. If he could work his way sufficiently close to make a sudden dash for the tent.... If he could get a gun against Taugman's spine, could overpower or capture him.... Yes, even if he could destroy the murderous fiend, America and all the world would be well served....

GRIMLY JIMMY started toward the marquee, striving his best to appear casual and unconcerned. Nearer and nearer... until no more than fifty yards intervened. Taugman was still there, still frowning morosely as he slowly paced the hillock. Then suddenly a wild clamor broke out in the camp. A shout of alarm, and now excited voices were calling and shouting, a wedge of men surging in from out beyond the cook-tents, carrying something between them—and finally stopping with it before a cursing officer.

Jimmy watched with narrowed eyes, knowing the reason for that tumult. They had discovered the body of the man he had waylaid!

"This costume—it is not ours!" the officer exclaimed as he held up the clothing Jimmy had discarded and tucked away under the bush beside the body of the German. "Ruppel was murdered, and the spy who killed him is here in our camp! Start a search for him! Watch that he does not escape!"

Instantly men started running in every direction. Officers shouted orders, companies assembled and deployed around the encampment—and then the yell that Jimmy feared went up. Out from behind a clump of bushes he saw Barlow and Jurgens—two of his volunteers—leap. A moment later they were joined by Shearer and Richardson.

The four backed away warily, their revolvers in their hands, but instead of losing no time in trying to effect escape, they whistled for the others. They did not understand, Jimmy realized despairingly. Knowing nothing about the power of those globular-lensed goggles the Germans wore, they thought their protection of invisibility concealed them!

And now Selkirk and Hargreaves came to join them… running straight into the jaws of death!

He saw the Germans closing in on them, saw the deadly ray-projector moving into position. And then he gambled his own life.

"Run!" he shouted desperately. "They can see you!"

But his warning was too late. The six doomed men tried to obey. They turned and scattered as they dashed into the gray barrens. But the deadly projector swiveled in a quarter-circle and its beam mowed them down, dissolving them into nothingness! Before his eyes they evaporated into space and were gone—and in an appallingly few seconds he was the lone survivor!

The instant he shouted, Jimmy had dived between two tents and then stepped out on a company street where he mingled with several dozen men who were running in response to the call of an officer. There was no pursuit—but the horror he had just witnessed had set his nerves atingle. The swift disaster that had overtaken his little band made him realize afresh the terrible fate that threatened all America. He dared take no more risks. His duty now was to return to his own lines as swiftly as possible and there bend every energy to a desperate preparation to meet the impending onslaught.

Cautiously he worked his way to the edge of the camp and slipped into the protection of a low clump of elderberries. There he lay flat on the ground and waited until the deepening dusk blended into night. Not until unbroken darkness had settled down completely did he dare to crawl back through the suffocating dust—slowly and carefully, until the sounds of the encampment faded and were lost.

Those miles of new-made desert now seemed twice as long as they were a short while before. Then there were six others to keep him company. Now he was alone—utterly alone in a world of gray death—one man pitting his puny strength against the destructive might of a remorseless horde equipped with such weapons as the world had never seen.

It seemed hopeless as he trudged wearily through the soft, powdery dust. There was no use striving for the impossible or flying in the face of the inevitable. The odds were too great. Those unheard of weapons were too all-powerful to resist....

But out of the desert stillness voices spoke to Jimmy Christopher—the voices of Barlow and Jurgens, of Shearer and Richardson, of Selkirk and Hargreaves. Out of the still night air into which they had vanished they whispered softly in his ear.

"The odds *are* overwhelming; the weapons *are* overpowering. But America has faced situations like this before," they reminded him. "When a free people must fight for their liberty, for their very existence, of what importance are odds and weapons? Remember the battling pioneers coming home to find their buildings burned, their families slaughtered. Remember Washington retreating from New York to the despair of Valley Forge. Remember. . . ."

And Jimmy Christopher squared his shoulders and trudged on with a new courage and a new determination.

WHEN AT last he reached the edge of the wilderness and found a car that took him to the American Army headquarters, President Warren was waiting there for him. Quick relief flashed into the Executive's tired, care-worn face when he saw that Jimmy was safe. Warmly he wrung his undercover ace's hand and patted his dust-coated shoulder. And then, once more, the badgered look stole back into his worried eyes as he saw the grim, tragic stamp of Jimmy's features.

"What is it, Jimmy?" he asked anxiously. "What did you find out there? What is this thing we face?"

Jimmy told him.

Swiftly he recounted what had occurred and outlined what he had learned in Taugman's camp.

"But—I can't understand it, Jimmy." Warren shook his head hopelessly. "I can't understand what an army of Germans can be doing here in America. We are at peace—"

"Now we are at peace, yes—and that invading force is here to see that we stay at peace," Jimmy cut through his uncertainty. "Franz Schnabel, we know, is about to embark on a campaign for the conquest of all Europe. He is taking no chances that the United States will come to the aid of the European democracies and turn the tide as we did in 1917. This time he intends to disable us at the start so that our intervention will be impossible."

"But, if he really intends to subjugate all Europe, why doesn't Schnabel use this terrible ray-weapon on his European foes?" the President argued. "That would quickly assure his complete mastery and put an end to all resistance before we could attempt to interfere."

"Because," Jimmy Christopher pointed out grimly, "Schnabel does not want a devastated Europe. About North America he cares nothing. Here the ray-projector's frightful power is to be demonstrated for all the world to behold—and to take warning. Here he will turn a whole continent into an arid desert as a terrible example to his neighbors—so that he can conquer Europe without the loss of a man and rule it with utter autocracy!"

CHAPTER 11
MARTYRS MOBILIZE

FEVERISHLY OPERATOR 5 and the American defenders worked during the week that followed. Day and night the great construction crews toiled on the fortifications, while in Pittsburgh a much smaller force of experts slaved fatiguelessly in a little factory that was zealously guarded. Daily reports came from the edge of the desolation to spur the workers on to even greater efforts. Like a creeping prairie fire, the desolation was spreading; was consuming everything in its path as it crept closer and closer to the American last-ditch line.

But now that line was nearly completed and was manned by thousands of troops clothed in the new uniforms Schirmer's factories were producing. Pillboxes and concrete embankments rose above the ground, tangled mazes of barbed wire and firmly embedded railroad spikes stretched in front of them—and from a distance of more than twenty-five feet it all faded into a misty gray invisibility.

Invisible to American eyes, but not to those goggles with which the Germans were equipped. Jimmy Christopher had not forgotten that, and on it he based the whole of his strategy.

That was a busy week for Jimmy—a week in which his head rarely touched a pillow. Back and forth he divided his time between supervising the fortification construction and working with Norman King and his staff in the Pittsburgh factory where a new and ultra-terrible ray-projector was going into production.

But by the end of the week he had the satisfaction of knowing that his plans had succeeded.

Deep underground, in a room on one of the subterranean floors of the great defense system, he met in consultation with the men on whom America was depending for deliverance from certain destruction. President Warren had come from Washington with Otis Staunton, his Secretary of War. General Lyman

Evans, the ranking general of the Army, was there with the members of his staff, and alongside Operator 5 sat Diane Elliot.

"With the new ray-projectors that are on their way here at the present moment we can meet Taugman's force and have a reasonable chance of driving back those we do not annihilate," Jimmy told them. "But that is not sufficient, gentlemen. It is not enough to wipe out some of them and let others escape. Now that we know our enemies are Germans, that force must be exterminated to the last man!"

He went on. "If we defeat them only partially, the survivors will radio home a call for help. That will mean war in earnest—an invasion by thousands more who will lay waste to our country in every section. We will have not one but a dozen forces to contend with, a dozen fronts to defend. That we cannot risk. Taugman and his every man must be obliterated; it is the only language Franz Schnabel understands. The total destruction of his supposedly invincible expeditionary force will be a salutary lesson to him and will put an end to his evil scheming so far as America is concerned."

"But how can we be certain, Operator 5?" General Evans' brow wrinkled worriedly. "How can we be sure that every man is eliminated? With this element of practical invisibility to contend with, how can we know whether or not some survivors escape out there into the wilderness?"

"There must be no survivors," Jimmy repeated emphatically, "and this is how we can make certain of that. We must yield these defenses, gentlemen. We must let the invaders swarm over the line and capture it after a show of resistance with machine-guns and weak ray-projectors which I have had made especially for that purpose."

"How do we know they will attempt to capture the line?" one of the officers objected. "How do we know they will not merely stand off and concentrate on obliterating it?"

"For two reasons," Jimmy parried quickly. "First, our fortifications are protected against the rays' destructive power and will not obliterate. Second, the Germans will recognize that we are using the invisible dye—through their goggles everything so treated has a blue-green tinge. They will figure that we consider ourselves invisible, will creep up on the entrenchments and attempt to take them by surprise when the first efforts of their rays fail.

"My plan is this. The army will fall back immediately when the attack commences. They will use the underground passageways to reach the hills behind us, and from there they will go to work with our new super-ray projectors. Those projectors, as you know, have overcome the resistance of the invisibility dye. They will be turned loose when the Germans are in complete possession here and will wipe out the fortifications and every living soul in them.

"To take care of any who might penetrate to these underground levels before the rays go into action I want these workings mined with sufficient explosives to destroy them entirely. And finally, after the line has been destroyed, our projector crews will close in on the wilderness area to pursue any possible survivors and wipe them out."

Heads nodded in approval and a dozen voices endorsed him heartily when he finished, but Operator 5 regarded them levelly.

"This plan requires men who will stay in the line and make a pretense of defending it," he reminded them. "Men who must offer themselves as human bait. Even though protected by their new ray-proof clothing, many of them are bound to be trapped by the deadly beams of our own super-rays and by the explosion of the mines which must wreck these defenses utterly. I need volunteers, gentlemen—a thousand men who are willing to lay down their lives for America!"

Jimmy Christopher spoke to the men at the conclusion of that conference. It was impossible for him to address them personally, but the amplifying system with which the fortifications had been equipped carried his words to every level and section.

"I want a thousand men who are willing to die," he finished that stirring call. "I offer you no medals, no plaudits, no hero's laurels. I offer you the prospect of certain death—and the opportunity to help preserve the United States of America and everything for which our nation stands. Those of you who wish to accept that offer, please give your names to your company commanders and they will be forwarded to me."

Hardly had his words finished than his desk telephone rang.

"Captain John Gardner, Company K, Ninety-fifth Infantry, reporting, sir," a voice rang over the wire. "We are in the line, and we have voted one hundred percent to stay here."

Company D of the Seventy-fourth, Company L of the One Hundred and Twentieth, Company G of the Ninety-third,

Company B of the Twenty-ninth, Company C of the Forty-fifth, Company J of the Fifteenth—one after the other in an endless stream. The moment Jimmy put down the phone he had to raise the receiver again. Where he had expected individual volunteers, whole companies were coming forward... were vying with one another for fear they would be too late.

A hard lump rose in Jimmy's throat and his eyes were suspiciously moist as he called off company after company to Diane. Seated at the desk beside her, she listed them on a sheet of paper and tried to keep check on the rapidly mounting total.

"We are way over a thousand now!" she gasped, as the stream of calls gave no evidence of diminishing. "We have nearly three thousand already—and *still* they are coming!"

And that took no account of those who could not wait to reach him by telephone, those who came hastening to the headquarters office to insist that they be taken. An orderly opened the door for them, and hundreds of eager volunteers came pouring in, until the big room could hold no more.

Making that choice was one of the most difficult tasks Jimmy had ever faced. Fathers came with sons, brothers with brothers—even wives came to beg to be allowed to stay with their husbands. Those who had lost dear ones in the devastated area insisted that that gave them the right of preference. Each and every one seemed to have a special reason why he above all others should be allowed to remain.

But gradually the men were chosen, assigned to their positions in the line and carefully coached in what they were to do.

Then they went back to their fellows—and prepared to meet the death that might come upon them at any moment.

At last everything was in readiness, timed and waiting only for news of the enemy.

IT CAME the next morning. Scouts came running back to the entrenchments from the deserted No Man's Land that separated the American lines from the steadily encroaching waste. From vantage points on the roofs of abandoned homes they had spotted the advance of the all-destroying ray barrage. Now it was moving forward with a speed and steadiness that was unmistakable.

The attack was coming! This was the supreme test—the test that would save or doom America!

Calmly Jimmy Christopher attended to the last details, gave the final orders and then rose from his desk to make a last-minute inspection of the front lines. But before he could leave the office an orderly stepped in to report the arrival of a messenger. The messenger, staggering, barely reached the chair that Jimmy held ready for him.

Ralph Kennedy was on the point of collapse, but his eyes blazed with satisfaction as his fingers fumbled inside the front of his shirt.

"I have a message for you from Miss Christopher, Operator 5," he panted. "An Army plane flew me here from Washington with it—but I came within a hair's-breadth of not reaching the flying-field with it. They tried to ambush me—tried to smash up my car...."

Quickly Jimmy unfolded the square of letter paper and ran

his eyes through its contents. An eerie portent of disaster trickled down his spine like an icy raindrop.

"There is grave trouble at the Consolidated Chemical works in Newcastle—trouble that may jeopardize all America," Nan had written. "The factories seem to be in the hands of the enemy, but that is all I know, Jimmy. I am going there now. I will try to work my way inside and let you know what I learn—or, if I can get control of the plant, I will try to hold it until you can send help."

The all-important dye-works in the hands of the enemy! That was a blow as demoralizing as the deadly blast of the ray-projectors! And Nan trying to penetrate the place alone, desperately determined on a hazardous *coup* to capture it!

But the girl did not know the people she was fighting, or realize that she was hurrying straight to her death....

Jimmy Christopher's face was pale and a dozen quick plans were flashing through his mind as he turned—and sprang just in time to catch Kennedy, who had slumped in his chair, at the end of his strength.

CHAPTER 12
WOMAN'S WAY TO GLORY

JEFF DARROW'S heroic death was still a stabbing agony in his sister's heart—a raw, torturing wound in her brain, when the emancipated villagers swarmed over the Stockton estate and laid siege to the house. She had led them in that triumphant charge, but now her part was finished. Storming a veritable castle was no task for a woman, they told her, as they gently pushed her aside.

No, storming castles was not for women—war was not for women. Only the weeping was for women—the agony of seeing a father killed in one's arms, of seeing a brother die before one's eyes. That was for women—*but it was not enough!*

Through Ruth Darrow's whole being raged a fierce, unquenchable thirst for revenge—an insatiable yearning to come to grips with these devils who, in a few short hours, had robbed her of all she held dear. A woman, she was not supposed to experience those emotions; was expected to stand by and wait for others to wreak her vengeance for her. But this was not Ruth Darrow's way.

With hot, raging eyes she watched the scaffolding, nearing completion, up which the men would swarm, watched the preparations for the assault—and sought desperately to find a part in the attack. Storming those high towers would take a heavy toll of life; even in her inexperience with things military she could see that. Surely there must be some other way that the building could be surreptitiously entered....

That was when her eyes fell on a half-crippled old man who hovered on the edge of the busy crowd. Unable to do heavy work, he had been forced by his captors to perform ignominiously menial tasks; had been made the helpless butt of their cruel and obscene jokes. And now, even though he could be of no use in the assault, he had come to gloat over the downfall of his tormentors.

Ruth read the bitter hatred in his wizened face, and she went over to his side.

"You must have lived here in Stocktonville a great many years?" she hazarded, when he plucked at his cap.

"Yes'm—nigh onto eighty-five," the oldster mumbled.

"Then you were here when this building was put up?"

"Worked on it," the bald head nodded vigorously. "Worked on it from cellar to roof, I did. I was young and handy them days."

"Then perhaps you will know—isn't there some other way into the place besides the doors?" she pressed eagerly. "Some way that hasn't been used for a good many years—some way that has been forgotten?"

The old fellow pondered, and then his face lit up.

"By Joe, there is!" he husked. "Down in back. There used to be a drain ran down into the crick that used to run back there. The crick's been gone near twenty years, and the drain's been out of use since then. But it's still there—I seen it last summer when I was hunting a woodchuck. It's still back there."

Ruth's pulses leaped and her eyes kindled.

"We're going in that way!" she vowed, as the men swarmed up the scaffolding and the assault began. "We'll take them in the rear. All we need is a few men—a dozen will be enough."

She had no difficulty recruiting her storming party. These men had followed her in the charge from the village and now did not question her authority. Fifteen of them went with her and the old-timer into the fields behind the grim old mansion—followed them on hands and knees through the dusty, long-disused drain.

At the end of a trip that seemed interminable, the old fellow called a halt and groped in the blackness above him.

"Here's the grating," he wheezed. "Now if I can get it loose—"

That task was too much for him, but stout shoulders took his place beneath the old grating. It was rusted and wedged tight, but at last it gave—and they crept out into a corner of the big cellar.

Warily they climbed the stairs to the first floor, opened the door and came through it in a rush. There were only three men in the hallway—and they died before they could open their mouths. From room to room Ruth led her little band, and death trailed with them. One by one they secured Lugers from their fallen opponents, and in a few minutes had control of the lower floor—were sweeping on to one of the towers.

Only once did they meet with real resistance. That was when they clashed with a party going to the tower for which they were headed. The clash was short and deadly, and when it was over ten of the foreigners lay stretched on the floor.

One of those who went down in the mêlée was a young, well dressed man who caught Ruth's attention. Blood was staining the front of his shirt as he tried to get to his feet, and a husky villager loomed above him swinging a length of heavy metal pipe. The fallen man parried one blow painfully with his arm, but he knew that he could not resist much longer. The fear of death flared in his eyes—and then he saw Ruth.

"Stop him—for God's sake, stop him!" he begged. "I can explain if you give me a chance! Please—"

Instinctively Ruth reached out and grasped the villager's arm to hold back the death blow.

"Let me talk to him, please," she intervened; and the villager turned to follow his fellows.

"I am innocent—please believe me!" the wounded man pleaded desperately as Ruth's gun covered him. "I am here by mistake. I couldn't help myself—but they will kill me if I am discovered. I can't explain now, but please give me time. I swear—"

Ruth did not believe him. She admitted that to herself—and yet, for some woman's reason, she was moved to spare his life. Perhaps it was the protective instinct aroused by the sight of his bloody shirt—perhaps that he seemed cultured, well bred. She did not long stop to analyze. Her eyes darted around the room and spied a closet at one side.

"Get in there and keep out of sight," the words came almost involuntarily—and she turned to follow her men.

SHE WAS with them when they charged out onto the tower roof and came to Operator 5's rescue. She was there when the last of the foreigners went down and Jimmy turned, panting and blood-smeared, to clasp Diane Elliot in his arms for a brief moment before he charged back into the building.

Ruth certainly was not in love with Operator 5; she had no such feeling for him—but she fairly worshiped him as her country's greatest hero. For that reason she could not help the twinge of half-envy that went through her when she witnessed the fervor of that reunion. Nor could she keep her eyes from turning to him and Diane later when they were downstairs in

the main room of the burning building.

From his hiding place the wounded man she had almost forgotten saw that reaction, and made his own plans.... It was not until the building was blazing fiercely that Ruth remembered him—remembered that he had been barely able to stagger to his hiding place. Evading the others, who were rounding up the prisoners, she rushed back through the doorway and found him running from window to window like a trapped animal. He was panic-stricken, but the moment he saw the she had come back to him his composure returned and a weak grin lighted his face.

"I thought you were so

The girl screamed her warning to Operator 5!

dazzled by the glamor of Operator 5 that you forgot all about me," he pretended to chide. "You were so interested in him—and, of course, in the young lady he takes such good care of."

His twitting was sly, but not sufficiently clever to outwit her womanly intuition. Instantly she sensed that he had noticed what he supposed was her jealousy—and that he was scheming to use it for his own ends. And in that same moment she knew that this man was deadly... as deadly as a venomous snake!

He was not a mere pawn in this outfit; she was sure of that. He was someone of consequence. The cunning with which he was sparring with her, even while the blazing building threatened to come down on their heads, told her that he was not finished. He was planning not only to escape but to carry on after he had won his freedom—which was just what she wanted!

Storming towers was not woman's work, but there were other ways in which one could serve her country. Ways in which she could perhaps serve even better than a man....

In that moment she decided to match wits with this man whom she had intended to turn over with the rest of the prisoners... and by such a thin thread was the life of Henry Gerber spared.

"Get downstairs into the cellar," she told him quickly. "At the rear end there is an old drain that leads to a dry creek-bed out in back. The grating is off the opening. Let yourself down and crawl to the other end of the tunnel. I will come for you there."

With a quick word of thanks he turned and ran—quite spryly, she noticed—in the direction of the cellar door, while she slipped out into the rear and mingled with the rescued village women who were joyfully rejoining their husbands and sweethearts.

Jimmy Christopher and Diane left with the prisoners and a strong guard of villagers later in the morning, but Ruth remained behind to bury the body of her brother—and to pay a visit to the dry creek-bed behind the fire-gutted mansion. Gerber was waiting for her when she arrived. Swiftly he outlined plans for a getaway, and that night she rejoined him with food and a supply of water.

Together they set out into the barren wilderness, plodding steadily through the gray dust until dawn revealed the end of the desolation just ahead of them. Beyond that stretched a No Man's Land of deserted countryside, but at last Gerber found an adventurous soul who had returned to the doomed area with an automobile to salvage some of his belongings. Gerber paid him handsomely to drive them to Columbus—to a rooming-house where he was acquainted with the landlady.

RUTH TOOK a room next to Gerber's, and spent much of her time with him. His wounds were not serious, and she suspected that he was using them as a pretext to stay in hiding. The "explanations" he had promised never came, but she saw that he was working upon her cleverly, trading on her emotions, her sympathy, her supposed jealousy. Skillfully she played up to him, pretended to fall in with his half-veiled plans—and she began to learn more about that rooming-house and its occupants.

Mrs. Kirshbaum was no ordinary landlady, and her roomers were not of the ordinary run. They seemed to be foreigners exclusively—a group of three or four nationalities, judging by their speech. From her second-floor room Ruth could hear Mrs. Kirshbaum admitting them and greeting them, each in his own language. For there were no keys to that menage; all who entered had to pass the landlady's inspection.

On the sixth night of their stay in the establishment, Ruth noticed that the doorbell seemed to ring incessantly. Mrs. Kirshbaum had hardly admitted one caller when another was summoning her. Dozens must have come in, Ruth estimated—and then she recalled that Gerber had been unusually excited during the day, recalled a number of his remarks to which she had attached no particular significance at the time.

Now she was convinced that there was something afoot in the building—and at eight-thirty she learned what it was.

"Sometimes men talk and plan, and nothing comes of it," Gerber announced cryptically when he called her to his room. "But tonight you will see how things are made to happen. There is a meeting downstairs, and I am taking you with me."

There were more than thirty men gathered in Mrs. Kirshbaum's big cellar room—thirty foreign-looking men who eyed her questioningly.

"A new recruit," Gerber grinned her introduction. "She is going in with us—in the morning. I have won her over to our side. We—we understand each other."

In the morning? Ruth puzzled over the phrase, but as she listened to their low voices and watched their tense faces she began to understand—and what she learned appalled her! These men were the leaders of many others, the leaders of hundreds of immigrants newly arrived from Europe, who were organized and waiting for the word to strike at America!

As she listened, she heard news that was incredible—news that had been kept from her during the days she had been immersed in that quiet rooming-house. The terrible menace that had suddenly loomed over America had not been ended with the death of Kurt Mahler and the fall of his Stocktonville stronghold. Three days later Cincinnati had suffered the same fate as Canondale, and the desolation was spreading!

As she listened, she learned of the invisibility dye and the arrangements Operator 5 had made to have the life-saving compound produced in the Newcastle plant of the Consolidated Chemical Company.

That was where these plotters were going to strike *in the morning!*

"So everything is arranged," she heard the leader sum up. "Our men in the factories are ready. Our storming parties will each be in place on time. We here all know our parts. Nothing more remains but to give the word and take over the buildings."

Something more than that remained, Ruth Darrow vowed determinedly. It still remained for her to get word to Operator 5 and have this perfect *coup* thwarted before it could be staged! While she pretended to share their enthusiasm, her brain was busily planning, seeking a way to get her news to Washington. That house had been a polite prison for her all week, but tonight she would escape from it at any cost.... Even after their planning was finished, that meeting seemed to drag on interminably. At last it was finished, the callers were leaving, and Henry Gerber walked upstairs with her, took her to the door of her room and said good night with a grin that seemed to be at her expense. She was still trying to understand its significance when the door closed after him—and a key turned in the lock!

Now they were no longer pretending. She was a prisoner in a locked room, the only possible egress through a window protected by stout metal bars! All hope of getting word to Operator 5 that night vanished. But, she told herself with a confidence she could not feel, there would be an opportunity in the morning. Somehow she *must* find a way!

HENRY GERBER and his knowing grin were at her elbow the moment her door was unlocked early the next morning—and together they stayed there all day. Try as she would, she could find no chance to elude him. At his side she rode in an automobile to Evanston and had no opportunity to alight until she was in the midst of his followers.

Disguised as workers, they converged on the buildings of the big chemical plant from half a dozen directions—flowed into it through every door and gateway. Before the surprised guards realized their peril they were overcome, cut down silently and effectively. Before the amazed workers had a suspicion that anything was wrong, gas bombs filled the rooms with blinding, choking fumes that drove them to the exits—where muted machine-guns scythed them down mercilessly.

Meanwhile, the agents stationed within the building were doing their part with faultless efficiency. At the first sign of trouble the telephone lines were cut, the fire alarm was destroyed, the factory whistle put out of commission. Within a few moments every means of communicating with the outside world was throttled. The Consolidated Chemical plant was isolated so effectively that the rest of the city never even suspected that a ruthless butchery was being staged in their very midst.

Like clockwork that diabolically fabricated plan worked. In less than five minutes the shops, the shipping-rooms, the yards, the offices—the entire plant—were in the hands of the invaders. Quickly and efficiently the new crews took over the vats and cauldrons, manned the machines and filled every position that was necessary to the normal functioning of the plant.

Within ten minutes after the first guard died, the great works was operating again as if nothing had happened—but now the buildings were closed to the outside world. On the iron fences and in front of the locked doors big placards had been posted, announcing that twenty-four hour production was now necessary and that nobody would be allowed to leave the plant until the government orders were filled.

From an office window Ruth Darrow saw women and children come to read those signs and go away wonderingly—never suspecting that they were already widows and orphans! Desperately she wanted to scream to them and tell them what had happened, but that would only mean certain death for her, and perhaps also for any innocent victim who might hear her words.

Helplessly she had watched that ghastly slaughter—had tried to close her eyes to the horrors she had witnessed, to stop her ears to the dying groans of the stricken workmen. But always Gerber was there close at her side. With him she had come to the office, its desks and floors splashed crimson with the blood of the executives and clerks who had been cut down as they bent over their tasks.

"We are taking over the general manager's office, Ruth," he grinned wolfishly. "Three of us will share it—you and I and Emil Wessel, who will be my assistant. You will be my secretary. But let me remind you, Miss Darrow—" he frowned with mock-severity—"this organization does not permit personal telephone calls for its employees."

Gerber chuckled, but Ruth did not miss the significance of his subtle warning. Her telephoning would be watched so carefully that there would be no chance of summoning aid by wire. With Prussian thoroughness Gerber and his fellow-plotters had overlooked nothing to make the entire plant leak-proof....

To outward appearances the Consolidated Chemical works operated as if nothing unusual had happened. But before she had spent her first twenty-four hours in that office-jail, Ruth knew that things *were* happening there. Things that were kept hidden from her but that she sensed from the veiled remarks and knowing glances she sometimes intercepted.

Carefully she kept watch, using her eyes and her ears, constantly on the alert when she appeared to be least interested—and at last her vigilance bore fruit. For once Henry Gerber was careless and left the door slightly ajar when he closeted himself with two of his foremen in the inner office that he used for private consultations.

Ruth listened at snatches of their conversation—and what she learned filled her with utter horror!

Daring greatly, she moved closer to that open door, and out

from behind it came words that made her knees tremble. Those fiends were calmly plotting wholesale murder; were plotting certain death for hundreds of thousands of men—and chuckling at their grisly joke!

In that startling moment Ruth Darrow knew that she held the key to the fate of the entire American army—to the very existence of the United States of America!

But how could she make use of her knowledge? How could she manage to get it to the ears of Operator 5? A captive in that hermetically sealed plant, her lips were stopped as effectively as if the grave had closed on them—and yet she *must* find a way!

FOR DAYS she waited on tenterhooks, always on the alert, always planning desperately, constantly watching for the slightest opportunity—and at last her chance came. Henry Gerber had been very busy that morning—so busy that he had neglected to close the door of a strongroom at one side of the office which he always kept locked. It was still ajar when he was called to a distant part of the plant.

Ruth's nerves tingled, and her pulses pounded. That room, she knew, was used as a storehouse for a quantity of arms and ammunition and a stock of high explosives. If she could get through that door and arm herself....

But Emil Wessel sat in the way.

That was when the telephone rang. It was close to Ruth, and she answered it before Wessel could get up from his desk. It was a call for Gerber—but instantly an inspiration flashed into her mind.

"All right, I'll send him down right away," she said quickly and hung up the receiver, to turn to Wessel. "That was Mr. Gerber," she answered his inquiring look. "He wants you in the research laboratory. He seems to be very much excited—"

But Wessel waited to hear no more.

"Donnerwetter!" he gasped and yanked open a drawer of his desk.

Grabbing a sheaf of papers, he hurried from the office—and the moment he was gone Ruth leaped to the door and locked it. Just what had happened, she was not sure; it had all taken place too quickly. But one thing she did know—*at last she was in the office alone!*

Quickly she got behind a desk and pushed it against the door—then a heavy filing cabinet. Not until then did she dare run to the telephone. Breathlessly she called long distance and asked for the number Operator 5 had given her. For what seemed hours she waited for the connection, expecting to hear Wessel or Gerber come running back at any moment. Endless, frantic delay—but at last there was a click on the other end of the line and a woman's voice repeated the number.

"Operator 5—I want to get word to Operator 5!" Ruth spoke quickly, fearfully—for now both Gerber and Wessel were outside the door, were banging on it and demanding admittance. "I am a prisoner in the Newcastle plant of the Consolidated Chemical Company—where the dye is being made for the army. This plant is in the hands of the enemy. They are working day and night to ruin America instead of save it! Operator 5 must do something to stop them quickly or they will wipe out the entire army. Those new uniforms—"

The office door splintered and came crashing in under the blows of an ax. The filing cabinet toppled over, and above the desktop Ruth glimpsed Henry Gerber's rage-contorted face, saw the Luger he whipped from his pocket and aimed at her. It roared—but a split-second before the cartridge exploded she dropped the phone and dived to one side. Straight across the office she sprang and into the open strong-room, to swing the door shut behind her.

That room had once been used to store the Consolidated Chemical payroll until it was ready to be distributed. As a precaution against a possible hold-up, its heavy steel door was equipped with cleverly concealed gun-ports that commanded the office. Now they were a godsend to Ruth.

"Get back out of that office!" she warned brittlely. "I will shoot anyone who tries to come in here. I am going to stay in command here until the American troops blow this place down over your heads!"

"You fool!" Gerber raged like a madman. "You treacherous fool! Let your Operator 5 come here. I want to meet him again—but this time we will have a fitting reception prepared for him! But you—you are coming out of that room—if I have to blow you out of it!

"Emil!" he whirled savagely on his assistant. "Go down to Hoffman, the captain of the guards. Tell him I want dynamite—enough to blow this whole office out of the building!"

NAN CHRISTOPHER was sitting at Jimmy's desk in his Washington headquarters when Ruth Darrow's call came in. Ruth Darrow... for an instant the name was unfamiliar, and then she recalled Jimmy's story of the girl who twice had been instrumental in saving his life. Ruth Darrow was in grave trouble—her terrified voice telegraphed that fact with her first words. And as Nan listened her eyes widened with amazement and concern.

Twice she tried to interpolate a question, but the girl rushed on as if she thought that every moment might be her last. And then a shot put an abrupt period to her excited revelation.

"Hello—hello!" Nan called into the mouthpiece, but only a confused noise came back over the wire, and then silence that was absolute.

Quickly she tried to reach the Consolidated Chemical office by another line, but there was no response.

"Silence," she pronounced as she gave up her efforts; "and that probably means that Ruth Darrow is dead." Thoughtfully she turned to face her father and two of Operator 5's undercover agents. "But it seems incredible that a plant the size of the Consolidated Chemical could be taken over by an enemy without word of it reaching the outside. She must mean that enemy agents have secured control of the management—that they are committing sabotage."

"Stranger things than the capture of a chemical plant have frequently occurred," John Christopher contributed sagely; "and remember, Nan, she said that she was a prisoner there. Saboteurs are seldom in a position to hold prisoners in the establishment they are striving to destroy. Jimmy must be notified of this at once."

Nan turned to the telephone and tried to call army headquarters at the defense line, but it was more than ten minutes before the main connection was made. She was still waiting to reach Jimmy, when the door of the office opened without warning, to admit three purposeful-looking, foreign-appearing men whose intentions were unmistakable.

Instantly the government men went into action. Demaree's gun blazed as it came away from his hip holster, but the bullet went wild and a leaden slug lanced through his chest, another through his brain, before he could pull trigger a second time. Hutchins survived longer. Two guns in his hands, he threw himself in front of Nan as he blasted thunderous death across the little office. One of the invaders gasped and pitched forward on his face; another cursed as hot lead scored his ribs—but Hutchins coughed and staggered uncertainly. Blood gushed from his lips and from the hole in his bullet-torn throat… and the guns dropped from his fingers as he went down in a heap, dead even before he hit the floor. John Christopher barely had time to get out of his chair before one of the intruders was upon him. An invalid threatened by death whenever he attempted violent exercise, the old man threw himself at the attacker, but his feeble strength was useless against the husky who faced him. Once he managed to duck the pistol barrel that whipped at his head. Then it was cutting down at him again. He threw up his arm, felt the weapon smash against it with bone-breaking force—and the world dissolved into a blackness that was radiant with flashing, stabbing light.

Given a moment's respite by Hutchins' protection, Nan managed to yank open one of the desk drawers and grasp an automatic. But before she could get the weapon clear she was flung half-way across the office. Swiftly one of the burly intruders came after her, drove her back against a wall. His thin lips parted in a cruel smile as his fist lashed her head up and back—as his gun poised to smash down into her face....

But at that moment help arrived from a most unexpected source.

Over the shoulder of the bruiser who was about to beat her into a battered pulp, she caught a glimpse of a grim, tight-lipped face in the doorway—and again the room vibrated to the blast of the heavy automatic the newcomer had plucked from Hutchins' lifeless fingers. Mercilessly he shot the man who had trapped Nan—shot him through the back of the head, and then whirled to trade bullets with the remaining invader.

Ralph Kennedy... at a moment like this!

Silently Nan thanked her God for the patient she had nursed and then followed into a fiery trap that had almost cost her life. Kennedy had been haunting Operator 5's office, hopefully seeking a way in which he could have a part in the struggle against the ruthless bombers—a struggle which he seemed to consider peculiarly his own.

And now he had found it!

He was still weak from his wounds, but that did not affect his aim. His gun roared again, and the last of the intruders gaped at him unbelievingly and then toppled to the floor. Pale and raging-eyed, Kennedy looked around for more targets, and then sprang to see that Nan was unhurt.

"I was coming down the street when I saw those three hurry over here from that building across the way," he explained. "They looked suspicious. I could see that they were up to something, and when they turned in downstairs I followed them as quickly as I could. They were—"

"Spies," Nan clipped briefly. "Probably have a room in that building across the street. They must have been keeping watch on this office, checking up on our every movement—"

Sudden suspicion flashed into her mind, and she sprang back to the telephone. But there was no response when she spoke into it. Impatiently she jiggled the hook, but not a sound came over the line. That was strange. The three intruders had hardly had time to cut the wire—unless, of course, they had a confederate outside who had not come in to share their fate.

Nan's eyes widened with alarm and she snatched up one of the fallen guns from the floor when she heard the downstairs door open, heard quick footsteps on the stairs. But it was no foreign agent who came striding through the doorway—it was Nick Brophy, one of Jimmy's men.

"No use trying to do anything with that phone." He nodded to where the receiver still stood beside the instrument on the desk. "The telephone exchange was just dynamited. Made a complete wreck of it and killed God knows how many girls. One of the worst things I ever saw, dragging them out of that mess. Every line out of the city is out of commission. That's why I came down."

Washington was isolated, completely cut off from the rest of the country. Why? Because the devils who had callously murdered hundreds of helpless switchboard girls were desperately anxious to keep the capitol from communicating with someone—the answer flashed into Nan's brain. So that no message could get through to Operator 5—or to the Newcastle chemical works from which Ruth Darrow had just called?

That was a question she could not answer—a possibility that had to be covered on both ends.

"Nick, you stay here and take charge," she decided swiftly, as she knelt beside her father and helped him back to consciousness. "Kennedy, here is your chance to get into harness. I will give you a note to take to my brother—and then I have a very important date up in Newcastle, PA!"

CHAPTER 13
BAITED TRAP

NAN CHRISTOPHER flew to Newcastle and took a taxicab to within a block of the Consolidated Chemical plant. On the way across the city she talked to the driver, questioned him about the plant, but he seemed to have no suspicion that everything there was not as it should be.

"They're workin' top speed on account of these government orders," he told her. "Keep the place closed up pretty tight, too—but that's so that no spies gets in."

From the outside the sprawling buildings gave no indication of anything amiss. Smoke poured from the chimneys and the hum of machinery came from the partly open windows. Perhaps, after all, Ruth Darrow had dramatized her account and made it sound as if the activity of a few saboteurs constituted the taking over of the whole plant. Nan gripped the briefcase in which she carried the cloth samples, that were to back up her pose as a saleswoman, and approached the main entrance.

A guard stepped up to question her, but he was easily convinced.

"Office is on the second floor," he told her, as he held the door open and bowed her in.

So far there had been nothing unusual, nothing suspicious—but the moment that door closed behind her Nan knew that she had walked into a trap. Out from both sides of the corridor stepped men who seized her arms and jabbed pistol muzzles into her ribs.

"Better take it easy," one of them advised in a thick, guttural voice. "These guns—they go off very easy."

Upstairs they marched her and into a large office where an aristocratic-looking old man sat behind a big desk—a sharp, vulpine-featured younger man standing beside him. Nan stared at them in dumfounded amazement. She knew them—knew them well. And yet it was impossible that either of them should be there!

The old man was Julius Schirmer, the virtual owner of this establishment—the man who had volunteered its use to the government. He should have been in New York, instead of here mixing with this deviltry. The other was Henry Gerber, his secretary—and Gerber should have been dead, his body burned to a crisp in the ruins of the Stocktonville château!

"That is the way to handle a situation of this sort." Schirmer was preening himself to his secretary. "Not with bullets and dynamite. Never look for trouble until it comes looking for you, Henry. The longer we can keep the rest of Newcastle from suspecting that anything is wrong here the better it will be for our plans. Had I let you dynamite that Darrow girl from her closet we would have had the whole city swarming around here to learn what had happened."

He went on. "Besides, the Darrow girl will be much more useful to us alive—and so will our newly arrived guest." He turned an icy smile on Nan. "I cannot take time for you now, Miss Christopher—we are very busy today. But my men will show you to your quarters. We rather anticipated your arrival. Don't worry, I shall not forget you. I shall send for you—as soon as your brother arrives!"

"What sort of madness is this?" Nan flared as the guards started to move her toward the door. "What do you expect to do with me? And how long do you think you are going to be able to masquerade as one of America's benefactors while you are stabbing your country in the back?"

Schirmer's brows knitted and his mouth pursed reprovingly.

"So many questions," he chided, "and I told you I have no time. But perhaps it will ease your mind if I answer them. This is no 'madness'—it is the beginning of the end of the weak, stupid American government you call a democracy. Second, we expect to keep you here until Operator 5 arrives—and then let you welcome him, invite him in… to his death. And for your last, rather slanderously worded question—it will be only a matter of a few days before I am recognized not as the benefactor but as the *master* of America! Now, that will have to be all."

Unresisting, Nan allowed her guards to wheel her around

and march her through the doorway. Now she could see that there was more than the usual activity in the plant. Men were lugging sandbags to the windows and the roof, wheeling cases of ammunition and carrying guns. Preparations were being made to defend the place against the attack Schirmer feared. When that attack came Jimmy undoubtedly would lead it—and she would be forced to serve as the bait that would draw him into a trap that would mean his death and a staggering blow to America's resistance to Franz Schnabel's murderous invaders....

TO A windowless storeroom that was as tight as a cell the guards marched her. As she went Nan missed nothing. From the snatches of conversation she overheard, she gathered that Julius Schirmer had recently flown from New York to supersede his secretary and take personal command of the plant. But why had he come out into the open this way?

Schirmer was nervous and worried—she had detected that beneath the veneer of tranquility he affected. Something must have happened that had made it impossible for him to maintain his traitorous masquerade any longer—but what?

For hours she debated that question without result. It was still on her mind when she caught the unmistakable thunder of large-bore guns. The whole building trembled. That must be the attack!

Quickly Nan piled a chair on a work table that stood against one wall and climbed up on them, to glue her ear to the metal-screened ventilator outlet. Now she could hear the drone of planes overhead, the rattle of machine-gun fire and the deep-throated boom of the anti-aircraft guns that must be mounted on the factory roof. That must be Jimmy and his men, come in response to her message!

But taking this plant would be no simple matter. Schirmer and Gerber had converted it into a regular fort. To assault it would require artillery and thousands of men—unless it was blasted to bits from overhead. Trapped there helplessly between walls that might come down on her head at any moment, Nan Christopher hoped and prayed that Jimmy would decide to stand off and save his men.

But that plant, with its priceless dye-making equipment, was of inestimable value to the American cause. Operator 5 wanted to capture it, not to destroy it. The planes that droned over it were only for observation purposes—and to distract the attention of the defenders from the companies of infantrymen now closing in on it from every side.

JIMMY LED the first assault himself. With a company of infantrymen, he charged one side of the main building after a machine-gun barrage had battered out its big windows. But that assault was frightfully costly. As soon as his men were in the open a veritable storm of lead poured into them from behind the sandbags that were piled on the window ledges. More than half of the attackers went down. The rest charged ahead desperately—until he sounded the retreat and put an end to that hopeless slaughter.

On the other flanks, his lieutenants were having the same disastrous experience, recoiling from the frightful loss of life. Those windows could be taken—but the approaches to them would be piled ledge-high with bodies before the survivors reached the barricades and could use their bayonets.

The main entrance was far more vulnerable than that, Jimmy decided. That section of the building was built out some twenty-five feet farther than the rest, which placed it in a position where most of the machine-guns in the windows could not command its approach.

A hurtling battering-ram to crash in the doors, and then wave after wave of cold steel to clean out the defenders—that was the answer.

Quickly Jimmy gave the orders. Two telegraph poles were chopped down and dozens of eager volunteers manned them, grasping them by the footspikes on both sides. With heads down, shoulders bent, they charged—and the heavy oak doors buckled and cracked under the crushing impact.

"This time they will go down," Jimmy encouraged, as the pole-men fell back and prepared for another charge.

Once more those heavy rams hurtled forward—and the weakened doors splintered and were torn from their hinges. Ready at the head of the first wave of bayonet men, Jimmy waited to give the word—but suddenly he tensed, stared unbelievingly, and was momentarily rooted to the ground when his eyes flashed to the big window just above the doorway!

IT WAS Henry Gerber who came to release Nan Christopher from her narrow-walled prison—Henry Gerber and two of his men who seized her and marched her toward the front of the building to the wide hallway behind the main entrance. There everything was feverish activity. A squad of men were taking their positions behind a barricade of sandbags that had been thrown up at the foot of the stairway at the rear. Others were bringing them ammunition. But it was not these who caught Nan's attention.

Her questioning eyes were held.

On both sides of the hallway were lines of doors—closed doors that had been curiously cut away in the center. About three feet from the floor a piece had been cut out of each of them, from side to side, to provide an opening about a foot high—and through those openings nosed the muzzles of a score of machine-guns. At first glance the closed doors seemed to be intact; only on closer observation were the slits noticeable.

Every one of those deadly muzzles was aimed at the closed doors, Nan noticed—and quickly she visualized what would happen if those doors were opened. Attackers, swarming in, would see only the men behind the barricade in the rear, would concentrate their attention on them—and then be mowed down by the blasting fire of those concealed guns before they even discovered their peril!

"Exactly, my dear Miss Christopher," Gerber read her thoughts and grinned. "Quite a perfect trap, isn't it? We are just about to spring it—that is why I came for you. Now we—"

Suddenly the hall rang deafeningly with a terrific crash, as the doors quivered and began to splinter. The gunners crouched over the muzzles of their death-machines, and Gerber led the way on a run up the stairs behind those decoy defenders.

"I want you to get a good look at this!" he laughed tauntingly. "Up here you will have a box seat!"

From beside the big front window at the end of the upper hallway he pulled the curtains so that she could look out on the battle-ground. The path to the doorway was littered with bodies, but behind a barricade at the far side of the street she could see a company of men gathered around two long, heavy poles they were lifting from the ground—could see them come charging forward.

Again the building trembled as the doors shuddered under that terrific onslaught—but this time they splintered and came crashing down.

Nan heard them tumbling into the hall below. Then she saw the wave of bayonet men coming over the barricade, saw them getting into position—with Jimmy as their head!

Gerber's trap was waiting below—and in another moment Jimmy would come charging into it!

Horror seemed to chain Nan where she stood, seemed to hold her more tightly than the men who clutched her arms. But suddenly she shook off its grip—and shook off their restraining hands as well. She tore loose and ran to the window, sprang up on the sandbags that were piled behind it and smashed out two of the panes. "No—no, Jimmy!" she screamed wildly. "Go back—go back! It's a trap! Downstairs in the hall—"

Then Gerber was upon her. Viciously he tackled her and dragged her back from the window—but not before she had realized, with sickening despair, that Jimmy could not hear her above the wild tumult. He did not understand. He thought that she was trying to escape, trying to get to him. And Gerber's appearance there in the window had been cleverly designed to help give just that impression.

Instead of warning Jimmy away, she had baited him into the trap!

Nan closed her eyes and clasped her hands to her ears to keep out the blasting chatter of the hidden machine-guns that must go into action at any moment. A sob that she could not restrain welled up into her throat and choked her as she pictured Jimmy, down there, his young body sieved by that suddenly loosed storm of lead. *Jimmy!*

But instead of the deadly chatter that she dreaded, the building suddenly rocked with a terrific explosion. Then another—and another! Explosions down there in the hallway!

The walls were cracking and falling, the ceiling coming down. The floor beneath her was billowing up dizzily and splitting wide open in great cracks that were like glacial crevasses. She and her guards were knocked off their feet!

Nan got to her knees. Hardly knowing what she did, she crawled to the stairs and pulled herself to her feet—and then was almost knocked down again as Gerber leaped past her. Cursing savagely, he ran down the stairs, Luger in hand. Nan staggered after him, hardly daring to look down into the shambles she expected to see in the hallway. It was totally wrecked and strewn with torn, mangled bodies—but they were not the bodies of Jimmy's men! And it was the sides of the hall, where those diabolically hidden machine-guns had been, that had suffered the worst! The masking doors and the murderous crews behind them were gone—blasted into wreckage!

Only then did she see that Henry Gerber was clambering over the wreckage and making for a brown-haired girl who stood waiting for him, her face smilingly triumphant, unafraid. Mad with rage, the secretary's face was a hideous mask, his finger itching on the trigger of his Luger.

"So it was you!" he snarled savagely. "If that old fool had not stopped me, you would be in hell where you belong instead of making trouble here. But that's where you're going the moment I get my hands on you. Not with a bullet through your brain, you double-crossing sneak, but with my fingers in your dirty throat!"

With a leap he cleared the last obstacle and caught her, trapped her against the crumbling wall and seized her by the throat.

That girl must be Ruth Darrow, Nan realized. Somehow she had managed to come to the rescue and had sprung the trap before Jimmy could rush into it. Now she was fighting for her life; was desperately trying to tear loose the fingers that were digging cruelly into her flesh and cutting off her breath. But her strength was no match for Gerber's. Her face was turning purple and her eyes were popping from her head.

Frantically Nan went to her rescue. She threw herself on Gerber's back, tried to pull him away—but he flung her off savagely. Reeling away from his swinging fist, she staggered and went down in the wild tangle of broken masonry. One of the jagged points cracked against the side of her head, and her senses swam dizzily. Stunned, she tried to get to her feet, but her knees would not support her.

He was killing Ruth Darrow, and she could not stop him. She could not even crawl over there and grab him....

But at that moment the hall was suddenly full of men—men who came charging from every direction. Rifles were roaring and bullets whistled over her head as the grim-faced bayonet men charged past her to clean out the rear of the hall and storm into the factory rooms. Jimmy was there among them, was leading them until he sprang aside and dragged her to safety. And Ralph Kennedy was there, too—was flinging himself across the hall, to drive his bayonet deep into Henry Gerber's side.

Gerber's head swung around and his eyes were wide with what looked ridiculously like amazement. That was the first glimpse Kennedy caught of the vulpine features of his foe—and the sight electrified him. Instantly he yanked the crimsoned bayonet clear and threw the gun aside—to hurl himself at Gerber and pound his fists into the fellow's face.

Together they went down, a man who was mortally wounded and one who was still weak from wounds that had almost cost his life. Desperately they fought, as if they knew that only a few short moments remained to settle their bitter feud.

It was Ralph Kennedy who rolled on top in that savage mêlée—and when he staggered to his feet there was a look of grim satisfaction on his pale, drawn face. He had kept his pledge to the dead. That vulpine-featured murderer whose visage had haunted him day and night, ever since the Times Square outrage, had paid at last for the killing of Phil Dawson and for the mangling of Harriet Loomis and Evelyn Harvey....

ONCE THE main entrance was breached, the fate of the

Consolidated Chemical works was settled. Once they were inside the walls of the building, nothing could stop the onrushing Americans. From room to room, floor to floor, they fought their way, mowing the defenders down mercilessly or driving them out to meet the volleys of lead that awaited them outside. From top to bottom death cleansed and purged that great plant—but in the midst of the struggle the one who most deserved to die made his escape.

Julius Schirmer had dreaded an outcome such as this and had made preparations for it. The plane in which he had flown from New York he had kept fueled and ready, his pilot constantly on duty close beside it. And when he saw that the plant was doomed he left his men to their fate and took to the air before the victorious American could reach him.

Nan saw the plane take off from a runway on the roof and suspected the identity of its passenger—and again she wondered what it was that had driven Julius Schirmer out into the open....

That question was answered when Operator 5 came back to her, flushed with triumph, the chemical works completely under his control.

"Well, that's the end of it," he said with vast relief. "We've cleaned out the last of them. Now the problem is to recruit a new personnel and get these factories running again without delay. There is a good supply of the finished dye on hand and more—"

It was Ruth Darrow who interrupted at that moment—Ruth Darrow who staggered him with a blow more telling than any that Schirmer or Gerber, or even Wolf Taugman, had been able to deliver.

"That dye is worthless, Operator 5!" she called out, as she arose from where she had made Ralph Kennedy comfortable on a couch mattress she had dragged into the hallway. "It is just as worthless as the stuff this plant has been supplying you regularly! I know what I am saying. I heard Gerber and two of his foremen talking about it, and laughing at the fiendish joke they were playing on you and the American army. Except for the supply that was shipped to you for testing purposes, the dye this plant has been producing has not been what you supposed. The uniforms you have given the army have the quality of near-invisibility—but the formula for the dye has been changed. *They are not ray-proof!*"

That astounding announcement set Jimmy Christopher back on his heels. He wilted under it as if it had been a physical blow. The dye on which all his plans were based was invisible but not ray-proof.... But that was impossible! There must be some mistake! He cross-examined Ruth Darrow, tried to convince her that she had misunderstood. But she stuck to her story—and when he had a group of prisoners brought in and confronted them with what he had learned they admitted that it was true.

The American army bad been deliberately, diabolically, outfitted with uniforms that would be useless against the deadly rays they would have to face! The fortifications, painted with this worthless protection, would disintegrate the moment the rays turned upon them!

Convinced at last, Jimmy felt the very earth crumbling from beneath his feet as all his plans were blasted. Now, instead of having at least a fighting chance, those volunteers who would stay behind to make a pretense of holding the fortified line would be condemned to certain death!

If that news reached the entrenchments panic might result—but those men must be told. Resolutely Jimmy strode to a telephone and called the defense-line headquarters. Firmly he told General Evans the fatal news and ordered that it be relayed to the men.

"I want them to know what they face," he finished grimly. "And tell them also that Operator 5 will be there to face it with them!"

CHAPTER 14
DESPERATION RENDEZVOUS

JIMMY CHRISTOPHER flew from Newcastle to the headquarters where General Evans and his staff were facing the future with bleak despair. The main body of the army had already withdrawn to the surrounding hills, and the entrenchments were now manned only by the doomed volunteers. Out in front, scouts reported, the oncoming wave of destruction that had been halted for several hours was again in motion. In several places it had reached the line—and the concrete entrenchments had powdered into dust beneath it.

"We have failed," Evans voiced the despondent verdict of the staff meeting. "Nothing can stop this advance. It will sweep over the entrenchments and then will roll on over city after city—but before many more towns disappear we will have a revolution on our hands and the government will have to sue for peace at any price."

And for once Operator 5 could not gainsay him. The defense plans on which he had banked so heavily were a failure—and now all that remained was to die with the men who had placed their confidence in him.

Wearily he looked around that circle of familiar sympathetic faces, now crestfallen and dejected—and suddenly he realized that, in his intense preoccupation he had not noticed that Diane Elliot was not among them. Diane... where was she?

General Evans answered that question with a guilty start.

"So many things have happened—I have had so much on my mind—I forgot all about this note she left for you," he stammered an evasive apology and produced an envelope from his breast pocket.

Something was wrong; Jimmy sensed that immediately. These men whom he knew so well were evading his gaze, refusing to meet his eyes. There was something they had not told him, something they did not want him to know—and when he tore open that envelope and glanced at the folded sheet of note paper it contained he knew what that something was.

Diane was gone—out into that gray wilderness! "I know what the discovery you made at Newcastle means, Jimmy," that note told him. "Our plans have collapsed utterly, but you will not desert the men who trusted you. It will be suicide for you to stay with them and meet the German onslaught—and I don't want you to commit suicide. So I have taken the only possible course; I am doing the only thing that is left to do. I am going to Wolf Taugman."

Jimmy's jaws clenched and the flares of his nostrils stood out stiff and wide as he read that astounding line—and realized what it meant. She was going out there into that barren waste—was walking into the path of an army equipped with weapons that would annihilate her before she even came within seeing distance. It was a desperate attempt to reach a man who was as merciless and rapacious as the beast whose name he bore!

"Women may have a chance where men would fail in an attempt to cope with these woman-starved invaders, so I have enlisted the aid of five attractive-looking nurses whose husbands are staying behind in the defense line," Diane had written. "We are going out to meet the Germans in the hope that we may be able to reach their commander. If I can get to see Wolf Taugman he will put a stop to this destruction—or he will die by my hand."

Brave, foolish Diane! In her anxiety to save him she had gone to her death!

But she must be stopped! Already a plan, as desperate as Diane's own, had leaped into his mind.

"How long has she been gone?" he snapped at the assembled officers.

"Quite a while—more than an hour," Evans made uncomfortable answer for his staff; "and she took one of the staff cars. She made her decision almost as soon as we heard your news. We all did our best to dissuade her, but there was no use."

But Jimmy was not listening. Diane had an hour's start in an automobile; that meant that he would have to move fast.

"What are the names of these women who went with her?" he demanded. "I want to see their husbands immediately. Have them sent to me at the landing-field, General—as fast as they can get there."

WITH THAT he was gone—was on his way to the camouflaged landing field that was part of the defense line. There he commandeered a big army bomber that had just been given a coat of the useless dye. And there the five men he had summoned met him—five young men whose sober, resigned expressions told him that they had already given up their wives for lost.

Quickly he outlined his plan—and as they listened new hope sprang alive in their eyes. He did not have to ask whether they were with him; their eager faces had already spoken for them. As one man, they made for the big bomber, but before Jimmy could step in after them and take the controls there was another breathless recruit at his side.

"I just heard about Diane, Jimmy," Tim Donovan panted. "You're going after her, I know—and I'm going along."

Wordlessly Jimmy Christopher reached out and clasped his hand—and the cheery grin on that freckled face gave him new confidence, new determination.

Out over the gray desolation the big bomber headed, and in a few short minutes the civilized world seemed to be left behind them. Looking down into that barren, colorless wilderness, it was almost as if they had been transported to some strange, fantastic planet. A strange, monotonously flat land, utterly bare of vegetation, that looked like the sand of a beach.

Now there were ants roaming around on that sand—bluish-green ants as Jimmy looked down at them through the pair of globular-lensed goggles he had brought with him. Those ants were the advancing Germans—and Jimmy climbed desperately as he saw their ray-projectors turn up to melt him out of the sky.

They gained sufficient altitude to escape that threat, and in a few minutes the advancing troops were left far behind. Again the desolation stretched, empty and endless—until he caught a glimpse of distant buildings that seemed to be the enemy headquarters. That was as close as he dared go by air. The rest of the way they must creep forward cautiously on foot—with death the instant penalty for discovery!

In a few minutes the plane glided to earth and that little force spread out fan-wise—like that other little band he had led to their deaths, Jimmy remembered with a pang. But those six heroes had met their deaths because they thought that their uniforms rendered them invisible. These men knew that the outfits they wore would not protect them from scrutiny through the German goggles—and that they were worthless as protection against the ray-projectors. At least they faced death with their eyes open.

Slowly they worked their way up to the camp, with Jimmy and his revealing goggles in the lead. This camp, he saw now, was more substantial than the one Taugman had formerly occupied. Besides the tents, there was a long, low brick building in the center and several smaller buildings grouped around it. Now

Next instant all four had plunged into that pool of refuge!

the place was almost deserted, and Jimmy noted with relief that it seemed to be stripped of ray-projectors.

"That makes our task easier," he gave low-voiced orders as his men crouched beside him in the cover of a small stand of bushy evergreens. "We will spread out here and converge on that little building beside the brick house. Once we reach there, we'll try to creep up on the main building, which probably is Taugman's headquarters—and jump it."

THAT PLAN worked smoothly until they had almost converged on their objective. Jimmy saw his men creeping closer and closer, as they darted from cover to cover. Now the building was just ahead, not more than twenty-five or thirty feet from him—when suddenly the snout of a machine-gun poked out from around its corner and swung straight at him!

Instinctively Jimmy threw himself flat, knowing as he did that that would save him for only a moment—only until the gun muzzle could dip down and pour a stream of bullets into him. With a stillness-shredding *rat-a-tat-tat-tat* the gun went into action. Jimmy saw the death-blazing barrel start to dip—and then it was blotted out as Dan Driscoll, the man next to him in the converging line, threw himself straight into the path of the blasting lead!

Driscoll! The man could not even have seen the almost invisible gun or its operator. He had seen nothing but the flaming sparks that blazed from its barrel—and he had thrown himself over that to protect Operator 5! Death had shown only its blazing maw—and Driscoll had dashed into it!

Instantly Jimmy leaped from the ground and reached a position from which he could cut down that gunner. Twice his automatic roared, and the fellow dropped over the machine-gun barrel with twin holes in the center of his forehead—but not before he had taken the life of another of those blind targets. If only those men had German goggles....

Bending over the dead gunner, Jimmy slipped the goggles from his head and handed them to Tim—but now the camp was aroused to their presence. Apparently deserted a few moments before, it suddenly came to life. A score of men appeared from nowhere, and the air was filled with whistling lead. Jimmy saw one of his men go down—and then another. They didn't have a chance, firing at opponents that were nothing more than almost indistinguishable patches of gray mist. It was sheer murder!

And then he saw a way to stop it.

"The machine-gun, Tim!" he shouted as he flung the body of the dead gunner off the barrel. "Down on your belly, Hank!"

Over the prostrate bodies of his men that gun sang its song of death, swinging from side to side in an arc of fire and lead. Caught before they could turn and flee, the Germans went down where they stood—went down vainly triggering shots at the man who had doomed them. In a few moments not one remained. But Jimmy knew that there must be plenty more in the camp. They would come on more warily now—would surround him and cut him down from every side.

It would not do to wait for that.

"All right—up on your feet!" he barked a swift command. "We're taking that brick building now. Right through the front door!"

Up the low stoop he dashed and flung himself at the closed door. He could hear a bolt sliding shut on the inside—but the doorway was not strong enough to withstand the impact of that triple charge. It splintered, and the lock and bolt catches tore out of it. The door flung open and Jimmy pitched through after it—to see Julius Schirmer running in wild panic down the corridor and crying loudly! Squealing like a stuck pig, he whirled and raised a gun in his trembling hand—a gun that showered wild lead all around his target. Grimly Jimmy pressed the trigger and brought him down, just as footsteps pounded up to the building and mounted the steps.

There was a heavy table in that corridor, Jimmy saw in a flash. He leaped to it, got it on his shoulders and carried it to the end, where Schirmer lay—and set it up there on its side.

"Back here with me!" he called to Tim and Hank Wilson, but they were already running toward him, dragging heavy chairs to add to the barrier.

Behind it they flung themselves barely in time to escape the bullets that tunneled down the corridor after them. Jimmy answered those shots, and in a moment Tim and Hank joined him in a fusillade that cleared the doorway and steps. Again the Germans tried a desperate rush—and again six of them paid with their lives before the others were driven off. And still they gathered outside and came back a third time.

There was a reason for that amazing persistence, Jimmy knew—an important reason. Wolf Taugman! That was the answer; Taugman must be there in the building, unable to escape!

A GROAN sounded behind Jimmy, and he whirled inquiringly. It had come from Schirmer. The old man was not dead, as he had seemed. He was coming to his senses, was clutching at the bullet wound in his chest.

"Forgive me, Operator 5!" he babbled. "I am an old man. I made a mistake—I listened to Franz Schnabel's promises. I should have known better, but I am only human—and he promised to make me master here in America. He promised to set me up like his man Carliotti in France—"

"Carliotti—what has he to do with Franz Schnabel?" Jimmy demanded in spite of himself.

"He is Schnabel's man," Schirmer rushed on, grateful that he had caught Jimmy's attention. "Schnabel created him—backed him in France and England so that those countries would be undermined and ruined and could not stand in his way when he started on his all-European conquest. Carliotti was to have overthrown our government too, but he failed—you defeated him, Operator 5. But Schnabel promised me we could not lose this time. The men he sent me as immigrants were all trained, all experts—"

"And you sold out your country to a foreign dictator!" Jimmy spat at him in disgust. "Because Schnabel promised to make you a puppet boss, you connived at bringing in the murderers who have slaughtered thousands of your fellow-citizens! You are dying, Schirmer—a man of your age can't take a bullet in the chest where I sent that one. You are going to your Maker—but before you have to face him you are going to do one decent thing to make up for a little of your rottenness. Wolf Taugman is in this building—and you are going to get me in to him."

Schirmer's face was ghastly. His muscles twitched, and his skin was wet with perspiration.

"Yes," he gasped weakly. "I will—I'll do anything you say, Operator 5—anything you say. Taugman is up there at the front of the building. There in no window in his room—he doesn't trust windows for fear he will be assassinated—but now he is trapped. He can't get out, and he has locked his door."

For a few minutes Jimmy had his hands full beating off that third onslaught, but as his automatic roared his brain worked swiftly.

"All right, on your feet, Schirmer," he ordered softly, as soon as the Germans were blasted out of range. "Get up to that door. Tell him who you are. Tell him that we are all dead and it's all right to open up."

The fear of death flared wildly in Julius Schirmer's eyes, but suddenly something else dawned in them—something that squared his shoulders and prodded him to his feet. Without a word he climbed stiffly over the barricade and groped his way uncertainly up the corridor. Before Taugman's door he swayed uncertainly, then seemed to take resolute hold of himself. Firmly he knocked on the panel—and his shaky voice steadied, took on a semblance of strength, as he spoke as Jimmy had directed. Cautiously the headquarters door opened. Taugman's gross face appeared in the crack—and his eyes popped wide when he saw Schirmer's blood-drenched figure, saw the man dying there on his feet! Hastily he tried to slam the door shut—but Jimmy's weight catapulted against it, snapped it wide, and flung the German half-way across the room.

JIMMY WAS in after him like a flash. He was on top of Taugman even before he could get to his feet—even before he could leap clear of the corpse of a young woman over which he had stumbled. A pretty young American girl whose dead fingers still clutched the weapon that had drilled a black hole through her own temple....

Red rage swept through Jimmy Christopher's whole being at the sight of that pathetic young suicide. With berserk fury he hurled himself at the German commander and ripped the Luger out of his fingers. Sending it spinning across the room, he met the inhuman beast barehanded, pounded his face with a fist tattoo, drove him back against a wall that was covered with a huge map of the United States—a map on which the gray desolation was a crimson blot, painted in day by day.

Taugman's skull thumped back against that map as Jimmy's steely fingers closed on his throat.

Vainly the man whose philosophy knew no mercy tried to plead for his life, but the frenzied words were only inarticulate snatches of distorted sound when they escaped from his tortured throat. Taugman's threshing struggles became feebler, his eyes were glazing. But before Operator 5 could squeeze the last breath of life out of him, there was an interruption from somewhere outside. Hoarse yells and the sound of running feet!

Tim and Hank Wilson were out there in the doorway, holding off the Germans, but Jimmy let the half-unconscious body drop from his hooked fingers and leaped back through the doorway into the corridor.

"The Germans!" Tim Donovan yelled. "They're coming back from the front—the survivors! Our boys have put the fear of God into them!"

Wild exultation rioted through Jimmy as he looked out at that rout of terrified men. His plan had worked miraculously! The line must have held long enough to trap the invaders, and then the super-rays had done the rest. These survivors were fleeing for their lives, running back madly to the only place of security they knew.

But suddenly it came to Jimmy Christopher that there was no security for anybody in that headquarters! After those routed fugitives would come the avenging Americans with the all-destroying beams of their super-ray projectors! In a few minutes that entire encampment would be wiped from the face of the earth as if it never had existed!

There was not a moment to lose! Diane must be somewhere in that brick building—if she was still alive. Frantically he dashed back down the corridor and bent over the unconscious Taugman, to snatch a bunch of keys from his pocket. Door after door on that corridor he opened—until a black cell of a room ended his search. Diane was there.... Diane and three of her companions, tied up and helpless on the floor.

Jimmy's pocket-knife made short work of the ropes that held them. But when he looked into Diane's trusting eyes a bitter realization of the utter futility of what he was doing overwhelmed him. Diane thought he had come to rescue her. But he was only giving her a reprieve—dashing in here to die in her arms.

There was ho hope of escape from that trap he had planned himself. They were doomed to be burned down by their own ray-projectors—by those ultra-powerful engines of destruction that would eat their corroding way even through properly insulation-dyed uniforms. At any instant the deadly rays that were his own creation would reach out and obliterate them....

THIS WAS the end—but suddenly Tim Donovan was there at his side, was shouting excitedly, fairly dancing up and down as he tugged at Jimmy's arm.

"I found their laboratory back there!" that irrepressible freckle-face was yelling. "The place where they manufacture their dye—the good dye that is ray-resisting, Jimmy! There's a whole tank full of it there!"

Dimly Jimmy heard him and caught the import of what he was saying. A tank full of the German invisible, ray-proof dye.... But what good was that now? The rays of the powerful American super-projectors would eat through it as quickly as through these uselessly dyed outfits they wore. They were hopelessly trapped, hoisted on their own petards....

But were they?

Suddenly inspiration dawned like a great light in the gloom that enshrouded him. A tank full of the dye! That might be strong enough—might resist even the rays of the super-projectors!

"Where is it, Tim?" he gasped. "Quick, man—every second counts!"

Tim led the way at top speed—led the way into a rear room that was fitted up with test-tubes and retorts, with carboys of chemicals... and with a great vat in the middle of the floor. A deep vat that was like a swimming pool—filled almost to the brim with the life-saving dye!

"Into it!" Jimmy shouted. Before Diane and the terrified girls could comprehend his meaning, he pushed them over the edge, shoved Tim Donovan and Hank Wilson in after them.

But now he could hear the panic-stricken Germans out in the corridor frantically seeking a place of safety. They, too, must have thought of that dye vat. They were pounding up to the laboratory door, had started to open it just as Jimmy flung himself against it and threw the stout bolt that held it fast. Wild yells of terror rang in his ears as he leaped back and flung himself into the pool—and then the whole world seemed to come to an end!

Wide-eyed, Jimmy saw that building going to pieces over his head; saw the roof toppling as great patches of the wall disappeared into nothingness; saw bricks and masonry come plummeting down at him—and disintegrate into powdery dust before they reached the surface of the dye bath.

"Down! Down!" he gasped a warning to the others. "Keep under the surface as long as you can—and when you have to come up for air just let your nostrils come out over the surface."

Hazarding his own life recklessly, he kept watch over them—caught them and held them when they would have bobbed up into the beam that had leveled everything up to the edge of that pool of dye. Gone was the building, the camp, the suddenly stilled German fugitives. Gone was every vestige of Wolf Taugman and the merciless scourge with which he thought to ravage and despoil all of America....

Not until the gloriously triumphant notes of a bugle sounding the recall rang out over the desolation did Jimmy dare to show his head, dare to creep over the crumbled edge of the pool and help Diane out of it. Together they stood there and stared out over the barren wilderness... stared sharply at the distant hills, where a huge American flag waved in the breeze.

No longer hiding beneath a shroud of invisibility, the Stars and Stripes were proudly flying over a reclaimed land—over a desert waste that would bloom again and be populated with cities and towns even more happy and prosperous than those that had once stood there.

"Thank God, it's over, darling," Diane Elliot spoke softly reverently—and Jimmy Christopher fervently echoed her words.

It was over; the menace was past. Now all that remained was the task of rebuilding. Lithely, with new, abundant vigor, Operator 5 set out on the long walk home... and as the miles of desert waste fell behind the little company of survivors his untiring mind was busily making new plans for the task that awaited him.

Author's Note: When Wolf Taugman and his murderous host of invaders were annihilated by the beams of the super-ray projector, their terrible menace to America seemed to be at an end. However the evil seeds they had sewn were to bear a harvest the unsuspecting nation little expected! Jimmy Christopher did not know, as he set about the task of rebuilding, that he was soon to face weapons even more terrible than the astounding engines of destruction already mastered; weapons that were to drive America to the very brink of destruction. The account of this thrilling adventure will appear in the next installment.

POPULAR HERO PULPS  AVAILABLE NOW:

OPERATOR 5

- ❑ #1: The Masked Invasion $13.95
- ❑ #2: The Invisible Empire $13.95
- ❑ #3: The Yellow Scourge $13.95
- ❑ #4: The Melting Death $13.95
- ❑ #5: Cavern of the Damned $13.95
- ❑ #6: Master of Broken Men $13.95
- ❑ #7: Invasion of the Dark Legions $13.95
- ❑ #8: The Green Death Mists $13.95
- ❑ #9: Legions of Starvation $13.95
- ❑ #10: The Red Invader $13.95
- ❑ #11: The League of War-Monsters $13.95
- ❑ #12: The Army of the Dead $13.95
- ❑ #13: March of the Flame Marauders $13.95
- ❑ #14: Blood Reign of the Dictator $13.95
- ❑ #15: Invasion of the Yellow Warlords $13.95
- ❑ #16: Legions of the Death Master $13.95
- ❑ #17: Hosts of the Flaming Death $13.95
- ❑ #18: Invasion of the Crimson Death Cult $13.95
- ❑ #19: Attack of the Blizzard Men $13.95
- ❑ #20: Scourge of the Invisible Death $13.95
- ❑ #21: Raiders of the Red Death $13.95
- ❑ #22: War-Dogs of the Green Destroyer $13.95
- ❑ #23: Rockets From Hell $13.95
- ❑ #24: War-Masters from the Orient $13.95
- ❑ #25: Crime's Reign of Terror $13.95
- ❑ #26: Death's Ragged Army $13.95
- ❑ #27: Patriots' Death Battalion $13.95
- ❑ #28: The Bloody Forty-five Days $13.95
- ❑ #29: America's Plague Battalions $13.95
- ❑ #30: Liberty's Suicide Legions $13.95
- ❑ #31: Siege of the Thousand Patriots $13.95
- ❑ #32: Patriots' Death March $14.95
- ❑ #33: Revolt of the Lost Legions $14.95
- ❑ #34: Drums of Destruction $14.95
- ❑ #35: The Army Without a Country $14.95
- ❑ #36: The Bloody Frontiers $14.95
- ❑ #37: The Coming of the Mongol Hordes $14.95
- ❑ #38: The Siege That Brought Black Death $16.95
- ❑ #39: Revolt of the Devil Men $16.95
- ❑ #40: The Suicide Battalion $16.95
- ❑ #41: The Day of the Damned $16.95
- ❑ #42: The Dawn That Shook the World $16.95
- ❑ ***NEW:*** #43: When Hell Came to America $16.95

G-8 AND HIS BATTLE ACES

- ❑ #1: The Bat Staffel $13.95

CAPTAIN COMBAT

- ❑ #1: The Sky Beast of Berlin $13.95
- ❑ #2: Red Wings For the Blood Battalion $13.95
- ❑ #3: Low Ceiling For Nazi Hell Hawks $13.95

ACE G-MAN

- ❑ #1: The Suicide Squad Reports for Death $14.95
- ❑ #2: Coffins for the Suicide Squad $14.95
- ❑ #3: Shells for the Suicide Squad $14.95
- ❑ #4: The Suicide Squad in Corpse-Town $14.95
- ❑ #5: Wanted–In Three Pine Coffins $14.95
- ❑ #6: The Suicide Squad's Dawn Patrol $14.95
- ❑ #7: Targets for the Flaming Arrow $16.95

DUSTY AYRES AND HIS BATTLE BIRDS

- ❑ #1: Black Lightning! $13.95
- ❑ #2: Crimson Doom $13.95
- ❑ #3: The Purple Tornado $13.95
- ❑ #4: The Screaming Eye $13.95
- ❑ #5: The Green Thunderbolt $13.95
- ❑ #6: The Red Destroyer $13.95
- ❑ #7: The White Death $13.95
- ❑ #8: The Black Avenger $13.95
- ❑ #9: The Silver Typhoon $13.95
- ❑ #10: The Troposphere F-S $13.95
- ❑ #11: The Blue Cyclone $13.95
- ❑ #12: The Tesla Raiders $13.95

MAVERICKS

- ❑ #1: Five Against the Law $12.95
- ❑ #2: Mesquite Manhunters $12.95
- ❑ #3: Bait for the Lobo Pack $12.95
- ❑ #4: Doc Grimson's Outlaw Posse $12.95
- ❑ #5: Charlie Parr's Gunsmoke Cure $12.95

THE MYSTERIOUS WU FANG

- ❑ #1: The Case of the Six Coffins $12.95
- ❑ #2: The Case of the Scarlet Feather $12.95
- ❑ #3: The Case of the Yellow Mask $12.95
- ❑ #4: The Case of the Suicide Tomb $12.95
- ❑ #5: The Case of the Green Death $12.95
- ❑ #6: The Case of the Black Lotus $12.95
- ❑ #7: The Case of the Hidden Scourge $12.95

THE SECRET 6

- ❑ #1: The Red Shadow $13.95
- ❑ #2: House of Walking Corpses $13.95
- ❑ #3: The Monster Murders $13.95
- ❑ #4: The Golden Alligator $13.95

CAPTAIN ZERO

- ❑ #1: City of Deadly Sleep $13.95
- ❑ #2: The Mark of Zero! $13.95
- ❑ #3: The Golden Murder Syndicate $13.95

www.ingramcontent.com/pod-product-compliance
Lightning Source LLC
LaVergne TN
LVHW090943080826
845145LV00003B/873